The Priestess Chronicles
Volume 3

Shiloh Rising

# Chapter 1

'No, no, no! Not again. Damn you Raziel.' Culaan looked around the darkened alley, but didn't need to see, to know that Ariela wasn't with him. Since he had acquired his mother's Druid powers, he had been able to sense Ariela when she was near.

'Seems that our winged travel guide enjoys keeping you two apart.' Genevieve smiled, trying to make light of her brother's frustration. 'Maybe you should marry the girl and make it official. He might stop trying to keep her honour intact then?'

'I haven't had more than a few minutes privacy with her since we began this *adventure*. How on earth am I supposed to get to the marrying stage?' Genevieve patted Culaan's shoulder and pouted in mock sympathy before she surveyed their surroundings.

The alleyway was cobbled stones and the buildings were stone, not thatch, all a sign that they had not been dropped in the middle of nowhere this time. At least she could find a good meal and some ale.

'We had best work out where we are and what we are doing here before we worry too much about wedding bells in any case.' A strange smell, like dead fish and something the Huntress couldn't put her finger on lingered on the air. She scrunched her nose, trying to ignore the odour.

'I'm not interested in wedding bells Genie. I just *need* Ariela, here, with me.' Culaan complained and Genevieve realised she could relate to her brother. He loved Ariela, of that there was no doubt, but Culaan had been a ladies' man with a frequently roving eye before he had met her and since encountering the Priestess, he had abstained—something he hadn't done since he was fourteen years old.

'Do we find a brothel first then?'

'What? Not on your life! I hate to think what Ariela would do if she found out I cheated on her.' Culaan paled at the thought.

'A brothel isn't cheating Culaan.' The Warrior raised a questioning eyebrow at the tall Huntress. He'd known Genevieve nearly all his life without knowing she was his sister. As best friends they had drunk together, fought together and helped each other find suitable entertainment, but he didn't expect such a crass comment.

'You and I come from a different time, literally. Ariela was a Princess. She was kept pure for the purposes of being married off in a treaty by her uncle. You know she won't see your point of view about this Genie.'

The Huntress repositioned her bow over her shoulder and shrugged as she started walking out of the alleyway. She untied her hair, smoothed it back into place and retied it with the leather band before looking over her shoulder to see if Culaan was following.

'I just need to find her,' he pleaded as he began to move.

'You don't need to explain to me. I get it.'

'No, you think it's about the rutting. It's not.' Genevieve's face said she didn't believe him. 'It's part of it of course, but being apart from her, not being able to feel her presence or hold her in my arms is worse than going without, well you know. It's like a form of torture.'

'You're addicted.' Genie explained calmly as Culaan walked up alongside and they both left the alley together.

'In love Genie. Not addicted.'

'Same thing.' Genevieve smiled knowingly as they both stopped to take in the view before them.

'The ocean. That's what else I could smell.' Extensive wooden decking ran alongside a tavern with a few rough looking food stalls. The smell of raw and cooking fish was mixed with stale ale and what could only be described as human waste—from one end or the other.

'I'm not smelling the ocean right now.' Culaan looked down at his feet and side-stepped a greenish, brownish partly liquid unrecognisable globule on the ground. 'Where on earth *are* we?'

The ships that were pulled up alongside the docks were like nothing the pair had ever seen before. They had two masts, hung with ropes and furled sails. At the top, flew different coloured flags with signals, no doubt of royal houses or those in power.

At the end of the wooden walkway, stood a huge stone circular wall. The travellers stood gawking with their mouths open until Genevieve finally found her voice. 'I have absolutely no idea.'

****

Ariela knew she had been separated from Culaan and Genevieve. Their powers were linked to her in some way now. She had not had the chance to discover to what extent and that frustrated her nearly as much as being on another divine mission *without* Culaan by her side.

'Why Raziel? Why do you keep us apart?'

Ophelia giggled from the shadows and Ariela spun around to see her new friend pushing herself to her feet below a tall evergreen tree.

'What's so funny?'

'Your hair. It looks like you've been dragged through a bush backwards.'

Ariela's hand flew to her head and she could feel the tendrils of hair which had literally been dragged from her braid by the swirling winds of their travel through time.

Just as the Priestess opened her mouth to make a comment, Ophelia turned a light grey colour and emptied her stomach contents onto the raised roots of the tall tree she now leant against.

'That will teach you.' Ariela smiled to take the sting from her words. 'It passes quickly and you likely won't get so nauseous next time.'

The Priestess moved closer and patted Ophelia on the back, pulling her hair back away from her face.

'You could have warned me.' Ophelia wiped her mouth with the back of her hand.

'Pretty certain I told you it wouldn't be pleasant.' Ariela smiled, recalling her last words before they left Reznor and the Goth warriors behind.

Ophelia took a deep breath and her nostrils flared. 'What I'd give for a drink of water right now.' She stood up and looked around, realising there was no way she was going to find water here. 'What do we do now? I'm new to this, remember.'

'Well I'm not rushing around like a chicken with its head cut off on this mission, that's for sure. I'm going to find Culaan and I'm going to have some time alone with him.' Ariela put her hands on her hips as though Ophelia had control of her predicament before relaxing, remembering it wasn't her friend's fault.

The Priestess redirected her frustration, looking up into the early morning light. 'You hear me Raziel?' She was sure he could, but whether he would oblige or not, she could not be sure. The Angel seemed to be determined to keep them apart and her patience was wearing thin.

'I'll do what I can to help,' Ophelia promised. 'Where are we?' She turned in a circle slowly, trying to get her bearings.

'*When* are we, is usually the most important question. We'll find out where soon enough.' Ariela heard the crack of a twig and spun round to find the cause. A hooded figure walked toward them, the rising sun at its back.

The Priestess's first instinct was to draw on her power, but that might bring unwanted attention. Instead, she reached for her sword, only to discover she was unarmed.

'Princess?' The voice was a man's and sounded deep and aged. The use of her title took her by surprise, but she told herself to remain calm.

'My name is Ariela. This is my friend Ophelia. We are lost, hungry and looking for work.' She chose to ignore the use of her title.

'I know who you are child. We've been expecting you.' The man pulled the hood back from his face, but his features remained masked by the rising sun behind him. 'Forgive me for being presumptuous. My name is Titus.'

'How do you know who we are?' Ariela took a step back, trying to maintain a safe distance.

'Let us just say that in a way, your mother sent me to meet you.' Ariela had repositioned herself and could just make out the smile on the man's lips. 'Come, we will find you some food and anything else you might need.'

Ariela had visions of her first travel, when Morrigan had been expecting her, but this time was different. This time the man knew her royal title. The Priestess looked to Ophelia to see what she was thinking.

'Why not?' Ophelia shrugged her shoulders and began to follow. 'I'm hungry and we both know you can look after yourself if you need to.'

Ariela took a breath and slung the bag of relics over her shoulder, wondering again where her sword had gone.

'We thank you for your hospitality.' Ariela waved her hand palm-up to encourage the man to lead the way.

He bowed before turning. 'It is my duty and my pleasure your highness.'

'On that note. Probably best not to use that title here.' The man turned and nodded as he continued to lead them from the forest. 'If you know who I am, you must understand where I come from.'

'We will talk soon. Food, warmth and you could probably do with some rest. When did you last sleep?'

Ariela had not really considered it, but she was tired. She had been awake the entire day before they left, without any rest, and with a new day dawning, she was feeling exhaustion settling in.

Chapter 2

Genevieve forced her mouth shut and nudged Culaan in the ribs so he would do the same. 'We look like a couple of village children. I'm hungry, let's get some food.'

Culaan put his hand inside the pocket of his trousers, only to discover he wasn't wearing what he had left Reznor's village in. He patted himself down as though he were trying to find an injury. His hand hit a bulge inside his vest and he sighed with relief as he heard the jingle of metal.

'We have some coin… let's find some food, but I'm not eating fish. That smell turns my stomach.'

Culaan began to walk toward the tavern but was struck in the shoulder by a heavy-set sailor with a long, greasy beard, parted and twirled in the corners.

'Look out you rat,' the man grumbled and shoved Culaan as he made to move on.

Culaan felt for his coin immediately and grabbed the man by the arm as soon as he realised it was missing. 'Wait up there, *friend*. Could you possibly help us with some directions?'

The man looked down at Culaan's hand on his arm and frowned, as though contemplating what to do next.

'You might want to give me back my coin while we chat.' Culaan's lips turned into a forced grin. The man eyed the Warrior's hand once more, then his gaze followed up Culaan's arm, over the charcoal tattoos and the strong muscles until it came to his eyes.

The sailor reached inside his pocket and pulled out the coin bag without taking his eyes from the Warrior before him.

He passed it to Culaan without a word and then made to move away, but the Warrior held his arm fast. The man tensed, preparing to fight his way free.

'We are looking for some work. Maybe you might know of a crew looking for guards or fighters?'

The sailor relaxed and looked over his shoulder, scanning the area as he considered Culaan's question. He looked Genevieve up and down and smiled.

'There is plenty of work for her, but not on any ship here.'

Genevieve moved forward and touched the man's chest with her pointed finger. 'I can hold my own with *any* man on *any* ship.'

Culaan smiled as the man seemed to regain his confidence. 'There is no captain likely to take you to sea. You'd cause too much of a ruckus with the crew fighting over who takes you first. It just isn't going to happen.' The man looked truly apologetic.

'You point me in the right direction and let *me* have that conversation with the Captain.' Genevieve touched the dagger at her side to emphasize her point.

'No skin off my nose I s'pose. Be my guest. That dark ship at the end of the dock is your best bet.'

'Whose ship is it?' Culaan looked at the vessel as he waited for the answer. It was massive, with at least a hundred oars visible on one side alone. The masts were twice the height of any other ship at the dock and a dark blue canopy covered the deck, flapping gently in the breeze. Only two guards stood at the base of the gangplank. The deck appeared otherwise deserted.

'The King's. He might take a liking to your friend here and employ you just for the view.' The man smiled, nodded to Genevieve and moved on without further comment.

'That was a nice save.' Genevieve watched the man retreat. 'How did you know he took the coin?'

'It must be my godlike instincts.' Culaan shrugged and smiled mischievously.

'Well come on then Thor. Let's find some food and then visit our royal captain.'

Culaan led the way as they moved past the tavern and down the wharf toward the royal ship. They passed two stalls selling fish soup and fish fritters, but the third stall drew Culaan along with the scent of roast meat. His stomach growled aloud and Genevieve laughed.

They gently forced their way through the crowded wharf to find the stall keeper already handing two rolls filled with greasy meat dripping with fat and gravy to Genevieve. Culaan's mouth was watering as he pulled out a coin and handed it to the cook. The man took it, looked at it with a frown and bit down on it.

'What's this then?' He held it up for Culaan to explain.

'Payment. What does it look like?' Genevieve answered the question, then thought she should have batted her eyelashes or done something like Ophelia would do, but shook the idea aside.

The stall keeper started shouting incoherently and two armed guards rushed around the corner as though there were a fire.

'Arrest these two,' he yelled, as his face grew red with anger.

The soldiers looked at one another and moved forward cautiously. Genevieve dropped the rolls on the ground, regretfully looking at them as she pulled her bow from her shoulder. Culaan drew his sword, allowing a small flash of the weapon's power to pulse but not ignite. The light show had the intended effect and both guards slowed their advance.

'Hold on boys. I think we just have a misunderstanding here. My friend and I have travelled far and wide. Our coin is not local, that is all.'

'It is fake silver! That's what it is,' the round little store keeper protested.

'I assure you sir, it is real silver.' The man bit down again and took a few more moments this time. He drew his dagger from his sheath and scratched the surface, trying to rub the colour from the outside.

'Well I'll be. It *is* real. False alarm boys.' The stall holder waved his hand for the guards to move on, as though they were his personal servants.

The guards grumbled until the cook passed them two heavily laden rolls and sent them on their way.

'This is enough silver to buy my entire operation. Here. Take another roll.' He handed a roll over the counter. 'Is there anything else I can help you with? The chubby little man's face beamed behind his long, unkempt beard.

'I'm looking for a friend. She is about this tall,' Culaan put his hand to his shoulder, 'almost black hair, dark brown eyes and strong for her size.'

The stall holder handed a roll to Culaan and scrunched his face as he considered the description. 'No. Not seen her. Sorry. Don't get many ladies on the docks this time of day.' He shook his head.

'Damn.' Culaan reached for the roll. 'Thanks anyway. What's your name?'

'Matias, but my friends call me Tias. Where are you heading?'

'To that ship over there.' Culaan took a bite from his roll and nodded toward the large, dark vessel.

Matias bent over the counter and indicated with his finger for Culaan to lean in. 'The King is mad you know.'

Genevieve moved in closer conspiratorially to listen in. 'I would look for another place to work if I were you.'

'Sounds like the right place for us.' The Huntress smiled through her mouthful of food.

'It does, doesn't it?' Culaan grinned and returned his attention to the stall holder. 'Thank you for your good counsel my friend. We need ears around this new place. Do you think that silver buys us a little information?'

Matias rubbed his chin through his thick beard and took a deep breath. 'Well I'll do what I can, without risking my head that is.'

'That sounds like a fair deal.' Culaan lifted his last mouthful of food in salute. 'Thanks for the meal Tias. We'll be seeing you again soon.'

The Huntress and Warrior moved off toward the mad King's ship as Matias rolled the silver coin across his knuckles and flipped it into the air.

# Chapter 3

Ariela followed Titus out of the forest and into the rising sun. The air was moist with early morning dew and the Priestess's feet were growing cool with the dampness.

'So where are we Titus?' Ariela asked as their guide slowed, making his way up a steep incline.

As though in answer, the moist air grew in strength the closer they got to the top of the hill. The taste of salt touched Ariela's lips as the sea mist drew in around the girls.

Ophelia took in a sharp breath as the view gave way to an unending ocean. The port below was bustling, even at this early hour. A large circular harbour made of stone housed docked ships, while others bobbed along the wharf, waiting for their crews to board and set sail.

'This is Carthage, Princ…. Ariela.' Titus smiled as he forced himself to use the Princess's name, not her title.

'Carthage?' Ariela repeated. 'Why do you believe we are here?'

Titus shrugged as he drew two cloaks from a bag he had slung over his shoulder. 'You might have been expected Priestess, but that's as far as my knowledge goes. It's my duty to see you safely to our friends. The rest is up to you.'

Ariela looked over her shoulder at Ophelia with a questioning gaze. 'Did you know I was coming last time?'

Ophelia shook her head. 'No idea. What is the year Titus?'

'It is four hundred and eighty-three years since the year of our Lord my dear.'

'Your Lord?' Ariela turned back to Titus who had stopped to answer Ophelia's question.

'Yes. Since the Christ child was born.'

'Looks like we have a lot of history to catch up on. Who is the Christ child?' Ophelia frowned as Titus handed the cloaks to the girls and indicated for them to put them on.

'We can talk more when we get back to the village.' Titus turned to continue his way down the slope.

'What are these for?' Ariela asked as she draped the rough brown fabric over her shoulders.

'To keep you hidden. Put the hood up, both of you. We can't let anyone see you arriving.'

Ariela did as she was asked, forcing the many questions running through her mind aside as she followed Titus. He moved well for his age and Ariela had to work to keep up with him.

The forest and slope fell away behind them as they made their way down a cobbled stone pathway. It was bordered by a steep ledge on one side and a stone wall on the other.

Ariela ran her hand along the rough stone, feeling a little home sick for the first time since leaving Shiloh. The walls made her think of the fortress where she had grown up. The fields of olive trees and goat herds outside Shiloh were fenced by similar stone walls.

As they drew closer to the moored ships, the sound of cargo being loaded and armed men grew louder.

The small group circled around the wharf area and took a dark alleyway that the morning sun had not yet found. Ariela began to wonder if following Titus blindly was such a good idea, but the man knew too much about her to not be trusted.

A tired looking woman in her middle years eyed the girls suspiciously as they moved down the dirty alley, keeping their faces hidden below their hoods.

The woman wore clothing close to rags and Ariela suddenly felt the need to find a coin she knew she did not have.

For a fleeting moment, the Priestess felt Culaan's presence, but the sensation was gone almost as soon as it arrived. She stopped and turned to look behind her, but there was no one there except the poor woman.

'What is it?' Ophelia stopped and took a step back to see what her friend could see. She peered past the woman frowning.

'I felt Culaan, for just a moment, but the feeling is gone now.' Ariela turned to continue following Titus. 'I'll find him later. At least I know he is alright.'

'Was Genevieve with him?'

'I'm not sure. My connection to Culaan is stronger and it overshadows almost everything else.'

'That makes sense.' Ophelia offered a sympathetic smile as the two young women caught up with Titus.

'These aren't the most suitable surroundings for young ladies but it is where we hide in plain sight.'

'You have enemies?' Ariela followed Titus inside, now more confused than ever and wanting to know urgently what she had missed in the last few hundred years.

Inside, the tavern was full of smoke from the fire and the smell of stale ale and sweat wafted out the door as they entered. The establishment was unusually full for a morning and Ariela wondered if the ale was served all day.

She looked around and decided to keep the question to herself. Two men, likely only a few years older than herself lay with their heads back, mouths open and the sound of snoring coming from their lips. One snorted in his sleep and nearly awoke with the sound, but sniffed and fell back into unconsciousness without batting an eye.

'Please follow me.' Titus seemed embarrassed, but the sight of the two men only made Ariela think of Culaan and the first night they had met. He had drunken himself into a similar stupor but it had done nothing to dull her attraction to him. The Priestess scolded herself silently for letting her mind wander.

Titus led them past the long wooden bar and through into the cookhouse. A well-rounded woman of a similar age to Titus met them at the rear and guided them without a word, through a narrow passageway.

The woman opened a storeroom door and silently ushered everyone inside. It appeared to be a dead-end until she pushed past and pulled on a torch that lit the room. The lantern dropped to an angle and a shelf full of produce moved sideways, revealing a dark tunnel.

'Thank you Martha. Join us in a moment won't you,' Titus instructed in a whisper as the woman nodded and handed him a lantern from the other side of the room. The flame flickered in the light breeze that drifted from beyond the darkness.

Titus led them through the doorway and turned as the opening closed behind them. His face looked contorted in the glow cast from the lantern and his eyes seemed larger than they had in the daylight.

'Won't be much further ladies. I'm sorry for all the secrecy but these are troubled times.' He turned and continued down the damp stone hallway. The girls followed the dancing shadows cast by his lantern

'What type of trouble?' Ariela asked the shadow she followed, a feeling of mild claustrophobia slowly rising over her in the darkness.

'Everything will be explained soon enough.' Titus opened a doorway at the end of the long, damp passageway and bright daylight struck the surprised girls. The room was warm, with a fire burning in the hearth and the wide stained-glass windows throwing almost magically coloured highlights around the room.

'Ah, your Highness. It is a pleasure to finally meet you.' Ariela spun round to see a tall, pale skinned man in long, flowing gold embroidered robes standing behind the door that had just opened to allow them entrance.

'Ariela, this is Senator Victorian of Hadrumetum, a neighbouring port city. The Senator is a member of our Order and can make the necessary arrangements for you to be where you need to be.' Titus stepped back with a bow as the Senator took Ariela's hand and kissed the back of it with great respect.

Ariela curtsied without even thinking about what she was doing. She had grown up a Priestess, without the pomp and ceremony of her Uncle's court. Meeting a Senator, for her, was like meeting with far higher-ranking officials than herself.

'You do me a great honour Sir.' Ariela smiled

'Nonsense. You are a Princess and a descendent of the House of David. Your Uncle is the line of the Christ himself. The honour is all mine I assure you.'

'You will have to forgive me Senator but there is a lot of history I'm not familiar with. You understand the nature of what we do?'

'You do the miraculous. I know, it is wonderful. A true miracle of God. You travel through time to right wrongs.'

'I'm not sure we right any wrongs Senator, but we do what we are led to do. Sometimes I wonder about the Angel's motives, but I left my family, only a few months ago in my time, to do what Raziel and God called me to do.'

'Who is this Christ you speak of?' Ophelia spoke up, having tried to subdue her curiosity for far too long.

'Forgive me Senator. This is Ophelia. She has travelled with us since our last journey.'

'Us? Who else is with you?' The Senator looked to Titus for understanding. The man shrugged as the Senator returned his gaze to the Priestess.

'Culaan and Genevieve, but for the moment, we are separated.'

'Does that happen often?' The Senator moved towards a long table and both Ariela and Ophelia followed.

Ariela shrugged. 'I've only travelled three times since I left Shiloh. The first trip I met Culaan and Genevieve. The second, we found Ophelia. Both times, Culaan and Genevieve have been sent to different locations.'

'What time did you come from?' The Senator pulled out a chair and offered Ariela a seat at a long ornately carved table, while Titus did the same for Ophelia. A knock sounded behind a rug on the wall and Titus moved to open the hidden doorway.

Martha moved into the room as Titus took a seat next to the Senator. She deposited steaming cups before the girls and placed a large platter of fruit and cheese on the table before them.

Ariela was unsure if they should continue talking with the maid present, but Titus nodded his head for her to continue.

'You know I never really asked. Ophelia, what year was it that we left?'

'I'm not sure exactly. It sounds strange I guess, but I was a servant and each day is just like the last. We have seasons of course, but no one is discussing what year it is with serving staff.' Ophelia giggled nervously. 'Constantine the Second was Emperor, if that helps.'

'Oh, this is so marvellous. Titus, what the Order has prepared for over the last century, it is real.'

Ariela grinned at the man's excitement before asking again what Ophelia had already asked. 'Can you explain who the Christ child is?

'Well, do you know anything about the new religion?' Ariela nodded. In reality she knew very little. The monks she had left the Emperor's son Constantius with, were of the new order, that's all she really knew.

'Good, well, it just so happens that Constantine canonised a book of writings about the son of God, the prophet of the new religion.'

Ariela resisted the urge to interrupt, instead, she nodded and listened as the Senator continued.

Ophelia raised an eyebrow and Ariela shook her head slightly. The Senator did not need to know that Constantine's son was insane and that it was she who committed him to care.

'The new religion has been called Catholicism ever since, and everything has been going along quite nicely really until, well, until the Vandal's decided to blaspheme the Lord's name.'

Ariela stood and moved towards the fire. She felt uncomfortable talking about religion. It had caused nothing but trouble for her mother in the past. She rubbed her hands in front of the fire, carefully considering what the Senator had shared. She had spent her life listening to her mother argue with the King about religion and politics.

'I'll have to learn more about this new religion it seems. In the meantime, do you have any idea why we might be here? You were obviously expecting us.' Ariela moved back to her seat and took a sip from her warm cup of chicken broth. She could only hope she had distracted the Senator.

'Yes. Of course. I just explained it. The Vandals. They are killing good, honest Catholics. They are taking their property like barbarians. They say they are Christians, but they kill anyone who does not agree with them. They say that the Father, the Son and the Holy Ghost are not one and the same. That the Son is not of God, but is a real born son and subordinate to God.'

Ariela held up her hand as the Senator's face became red and his voice grew louder. 'Senator. I mean no disrespect, but I doubt very much that I am here to discuss semantics about religion. I'm an Israelite after all.'

The Priestess smiled genuinely at the Senator's expression. He sat open mouthed in mid-sentence, a look of utter bewilderment on his features.

Ariela continued. 'I'm a Priestess, a woman who travels through time, aided by the Angel Raziel. My friends can shoot fire arrows and wield swords of light and I can cast fire balls.' Ariela drew power to her hand and created a ball of light as an explanation.

'If God wanted to set the record straight on who His son really is, He would have done it Himself by now. I'm here for something a little more tangible than that.'

'She has you there Victorian.' Titus chuckled. 'He gets a little carried away at times. My apologies Ariela.'

'No need. I think you are right. If the Vandals are killing and stealing then they are at the centre of this, but I'll need to get closer to find out in what way I can help. Can you get me into the King's employ?'

'Employ? Heavens no.' The Senator had regained his senses. 'You'll be a lady of the court, along with your friend here of course.' He puffed out his chest, impressed with himself and his brilliant connections.

Ophelia positively squealed with delight as Ariela rolled her eyes. She had run away from Shiloh to avoid court and the dutiful marriage that accompanied it. Now here she was, smack bang right back in the middle of all the false

facades of people pretending to like each other for political or
financial power.

# Chapter 4

The whistle wasn't unexpected. Genevieve knew she was dressed like no other woman in the region. She wore black leather pants that were tighter than they needed to be. Her soft leather boots were laced down the front and her long-sleeved linen shirt sat low over her cleavage.

She turned to the whistler and bowed her head, accepting the compliment whether it was intended as one or not, before continuing up the gangplank to the ship's deck.

'You're inviting trouble again Genie.' Culaan smiled as he spoke with a sternness his sister knew he didn't mean.

'Oh, but you know how much I *love* trouble.'

'That's for sure. Do you think you can manage to not cause a fight on our first day?' Genevieve turned and rolled her eyes and shook her head at her brother.

A guard stepped forward and prevented them from stepping over the railing. 'Invited guests and crew only. You're neither.' The man held a worn club in his left hand, his other rested on the hilt of his sword. He was tanned with years of sun exposure and his long, shaggy beard was speckled with grey.

Culaan stepped aside, knowing the man was seasoned and not wanting to draw him into an altercation. Genevieve took the opening and sauntered forward.

'Well hello sailor.' The Huntress moved in close 'We're just looking for some work. I'm sure the Captain will be happy to see us.' Genevieve looked up to see a dark-skinned figure standing at the helm. His hands were on the balustrade as he casually listened in on the conversation below.

The guard followed Genevieve's line of sight, turning to see the man nod for him to let them pass.

'I thought so.' The Huntress rubbed her body against the guard as he failed to move out of her path. 'I might see you later,' she whispered and he chuckled.

'I doubt that honey.' Genevieve ignored the comment but wondered at the man's tone.

'Go easy Genie.' Culaan warned as he followed her over the rail and up the steps that led to the helm. One of the masts, the larger of the two, stood tall above the wheel that would steer the vessel. Behind the wheel, a cabin the width of the landing nestled below the top deck. The man nodded for the two visitors to follow him inside.

'You two are not from around here,' the man stated, as he relaxed into a tall-backed leather seat behind a heavy wooden desk. 'What sort of work are you looking for? I'm not in the habit of bringing a woman on board my ship.'

'Body guard.' Genevieve offered.

'You any good with those weapons? I could use someone decent with a bow.'

'I am the best *you'll* ever see.' The Huntress didn't hide her attraction. The Captain was tall, lean, but wide at the shoulders. She could only imagine what his chest was like underneath the dark shirt and woollen vest he wore. His skin was darker than most local inhabitants she'd seen and the scars on his face were marked in an intricate pattern that only served to increase his allure.

'Beautiful and modest. How about a demonstration?' The Captain smiled at her confident manner. 'Is she always this certain of herself?' The man's eyes fell on Culaan and he grinned.

'Always. But it's well deserved.'

'What do you want me to shoot?' Genevieve took her bow from her shoulder and pulled an arrow from the quiver at her back.

'Outside. Take your pick.' The Captain rose so he could get a clear view.

Genevieve notched an arrow and Culaan opened the cabin door to the daylight beyond. The Huntress didn't even wait for her eyes to adjust. She had scoped out the ship as they had boarded and she knew what she would shoot.

The arrow was released and thudded home as the Huntress moved out the door. The guard at the gang-plank turned, his sword drawn and ready, when he saw the Captain move out from behind the Huntress, holding his hand for him to halt.

He sheathed his weapon and looked at the arrow. It had struck the signet flag and pinned it to the top of the second, smaller mast.

The Captain chuckled aloud. 'Nicely done. Are you as good with that sword as she is with the bow?'

'Better.' Culaan grinned.

'Very well. We have room in the King's guard. You'll serve aboard the ship only when the King is on board. He'll be here later today. I'll introduce you to the Captain of the guard then.'

'Where is your crew?' Genevieve looked around the deserted deck.

'All in town, drinking, whoring, eating and doing whatever they can't when we are at sea. We sail for Malta on the morning tide.'

'We'll take a look around the ship then head into town. We'll be back when the King arrives, if that suits you? Unless you have other plans?' Genevieve's tone was seductive and Culaan cleared his throat loudly.

The Captain chose to ignore her innuendo, shrugging instead. 'Sounds reasonable. You haven't asked about the pay?'

'Any work is good work.' Culaan offered, but the Captain seemed unconvinced.

'Where did you say you were from?'

'We didn't,' Genevieve smiled mischievously 'but maybe I can tell you more over a rum or ale this evening.'

The Captain grinned and his dark brown eyes glistened with mirth. 'You two aren't an item then?'

'Heck no.' Genevieve sneered. 'This is my half-brother Culaan.'

'And your name is?'

'Genevieve but you can call me Genie.' The Huntress slung her bow back over her shoulder and winked at the Captain as she moved down the stairs toward the main deck.

The Captain questioned Culaan with a raised eyebrow and the Warrior grinned. 'Trust your instincts, that's all the advice I can offer Captain.'

# Chapter 5

Ariela tried to force her mouth closed as the small group was led from the meeting room, through a temple. The roof was so high the Priestess could hardly make out the colour of the ceiling and there were more stained-glass windows reaching up from head height, to the tip of the intricately carved archways.

The windows lined both sides of the building and between each one, a statue was carved in marble. One was of a woman holding a baby in her arms, another depicted a rabbi having his feet washed.

Ariela had seen her uncle's palace and the temple erected there, but this was beyond anything she'd ever seen before.

A guard met them at the entrance. Ariela and Ophelia lifted their hoods back in place as the men ushered them into a carriage. The Senator offered his hand as Ariela climbed upon makeshift steps and into the covered carriage. She shuffled over to make room for Ophelia who followed her inside. The Senator joined them before a guard slammed the door shut and called for the driver to move on.

The carriage seats were plush, covered in silky fabric of red and gold. The windows were covered with dark grey curtains, causing Ariela to pull them back to peer out and try and get her bearings.

'Where are we going?' Ariela let the curtain go and turned to watch the Senator as the carriage lurched forward.

'I have a home in Carthage. We'll find you suitable clothing and make the arrangements to introduce you to Huneric's court.'

'I think we'll need to catch up a little on recent history first.' Ariela looked at Ophelia who nodded agreement.

'Yes of course. I'll have one of the Priestesses from the Order help.'

'Priestesses? There are more here?' Ariela smiled and tried to subdue her own excitement.

'Yes, of course. Your mother's legacy has prevailed through time. The Shiloh Order of which you belonged is still flourishing. That's why we know of you and your mission.'

Ariela laughed aloud and the Senator frowned in confusion. She held up a hand. 'I'm sorry Senator. It's just funny because when I left Shiloh, recently in my mind, my mother and father were still fighting about letting me go on a mission at all and my uncle had promised me in marriage to broker peace.'

The Senator was struck silent a moment and then found the irony in his statement. 'Yes,' he chuckled, 'I can see how you would find that funny.'

'It seemed God had other plans all along. How did my mother die?' The question left Ariela's lips before it had even formed in her own thoughts.

'I think now is not the time to discuss it my dear. I can see it might upset you. We'll go over the history of the Order, including your family, once we have you settled in my home.'

Ophelia looked at Ariela and could see she was ready to push the point. 'Who are we to say we are, if anyone asks?' She patted Ariela's hand firmly, holding it in place as the Priestess tried to raise it in protest.

'My niece and her most trusted childhood friend,' the Senator smiled. 'You can use your real names. There is no reason anyone will be suspicious.'

The carriage drew to a halt and the girls, neither of whom were used to such transport, nearly fell from their seats. Both grabbed the window frames to balance themselves. The Senator chuckled. 'You'll get used to it.'

The door opened and a guard held his hand up to help the Senator exit. The Senator in turn helped the ladies from the carriage. The group moved between four guards and Ariela watched closely as they surveyed the grounds before the Senator entered.

'You fear for your life Senator?' Ariela whispered so no one else could hear.

The man shook his head, but Ariela was unsure if the motion meant no, or the Senator was unwilling to discuss it.

A tall athletic woman moved toward them as they made their way along the garden path that led to the main entrance. She bowed her head to the Senator and then to Ariela. There was a familiarity about her and Ariela assumed she was a Priestess of her mother's order. The clothing was different, but the training was there, hidden behind the woman's intense gaze.

The Senator led the group inside before removing his embroidered robe and allowing a servant to untie his sandals. The same servant took Ophelia's and Ariela's robes and then opened a large orange door that led from the enclosed courtyard to the main entry.

A fountain gurgled in the centre of an indoor garden. Hanging plants fell from the roof like living, green, waterfalls and there were flowers blooming in large clay pots around the room.

Servants flowed from doorways and the girls were almost overcome with attention. They were escorted up a grand marble staircase to the next level. Ophelia was led one way, while Ariela was guided by the woman who greeted them at the entrance.

She looked down the stairs to see the Senator smile and nod that everything was alright, but her instincts were screaming at her to resist being separated from Ophelia.

'Your Highness. It is an honour to be at your service.' The reverence was genuine, but it took all the Priestess's strength to remain calm. The Angel had led her here. These people were trained by her mother's Order. Everything would be fine. She had to keep reminding herself to remain calm, but something just didn't feel right.

'Please call me Ariela.' She finally found her voice and the woman, likely ten years her senior, nodded her understanding.

'My name is Idris. I am at your service.'

'Good to know. All I need right now is a hot bath and some clean clothes.' The woman opened a door and as though she had read her mind, a steaming metal bath stood before a fireplace. A set of clean clothes was laid out upon the bed which occupied the right side of the room. A picture window at the foot offered a view of the ocean, which Ariela stopped to admire.

'I'll return after you've bathed Ariela. You'll find a tray of food on the terrace.' The woman nodded to a set of glass doors on the other side of the room.

Ariela shook away the amazement and pulled her mind back to reality. 'Where is my friend?'

The woman's lips curled in a gentle smile. 'In the room, next door. You'll be able to see her on the balcony soon. Relax, clean up and then rest. I'll be back later to help and answer any more questions you might have.'

Ariela suddenly felt like an ungrateful brat and sighed. 'I'm sorry. You've been most gracious. I'm just tired. Please thank the Senator for me.'

'I'm sure he understands.' The girl bowed and left the room.

Ariela looked at the steaming bath, but something teased the back of her mind. She moved around the bed, tossing her bag of artefacts on it as she passed. She opened the double doors and moved onto the balcony. Her breath caught in her throat as she surveyed the scene.

The harbour was full of ships, some small, some huge. An almost black vessel, the largest by far swayed in the distance and as she focussed on it, she felt Culaan's presence. A sense of peace washed over her for a moment before she remembered Ophelia.

She looked to her right, but there was no balcony. Her room was the last one, with the most spectacular views. Only one room was close to her, on her left a balcony was almost within reach.

'Ophelia!' she called out, hoping it was loud enough to be heard, but not loud enough to draw unwanted attention

There was no response, so she went back inside and looked for something to help get her friends attention. *Why on earth was she so worried?*

On a side table, just inside the glass doors, she found a vase full of seashells. The beautiful colours were blended together, with a petrified starfish neatly balanced on top. She removed two fingernail sized shells and returned to the balcony.

She tossed one at the glass, wanting to make a sound, but not break the window. She waited, then tossed another as

Ophelia stepped into view. The shell hit her friend between the eyes.

'Ow! What was that for?' Ophelia had wrapped a robe around herself, her hair dripping wet on the mosaic tiles below her feet.

'You were in the bath already?'

'Of course I was. We left Reznor's village having not bathed for days. We likely smell worse than the fish mongers down there.' Her friend pointed to the harbour. 'Relax, have a bath. No one is going to die in the next half hour.'

'I'm sorry Ophelia, I just have a weird feeling about this place, this mission.'

'Why, because you haven't had to kill anyone yet?'

Ariela pouted. 'Maybe.'

Ophelia took a deep breath. 'Lock the door, get in the bath and then come out and eat. We'll talk then, alright?' She waited patiently for an answer.

Ariela nodded and Ophelia moved back inside to her bath.

Ariela closed the doors and locked them. She moved to the main room and jostled the handle, looking for a key. It was already locked from the outside? She forced the panic down as she realised there was nothing she could do right now.

She decided she would keep it to herself for now. Confronting Idris might not be the best idea. She needed to find out what was going on. It appeared either the Senator, or the Order were not what they seemed to be.

The Priestess found a chair by the side table and placed it under the doorhandle before taking her clothes off and lowering her aching body into the hot water. She closed her eyes and spoke aloud. 'What have you gotten us into this time Raziel?

 # Chapter 6

Culaan stopped and looked over his shoulder, studying the skyline. Genevieve bumped into him as she hadn't taken her eyes off the ship's Captain while making her way down the gangplank.

'What!' Genevieve followed his line of sight toward the distant hills. She squinted trying to make out the buildings. There was what could only be the King's palace, a huge stone building topped with domes upon tall towers. It was surrounded by similarly impressive buildings, but smaller in stature.

'Ah, the rich quarter.'

'I can feel Ariela.'

Genevieve laughed aloud as Culaan moved on, the Huntress right behind him.

'What is so funny?'

'The Princess gets to stay in the snobby end of town while we get the dead fish smelling peasant quarters. Why am I not surprised?'

'You shouldn't be. We are working both sides of the King it seems. Besides let's be fair about this—last time Ariela was the hired help while we got to play at being gods, so it's her turn.'

'True. That was fun.' Genevieve slapped Culaan on the back. Let's get something to eat. That snack from Matias didn't do much for my appetite.'

The pair made their way to the tavern and moved inside the wooden building. The walls were thin, with gaps in the timber joints and the ceilings were low, with heavy beams making it feel like the lower decks of a ship.

The smell of roasting meat met them and Culaan's stomach growled in response. 'At least it isn't fish.'

They moved past two long tables full of sailors, some still drinking from the night before, some still whoring like there was no tomorrow. A woman, who wriggled and murmured sounds of enjoyment winked at Genevieve as she moved past.

Culaan found a small table at the rear of the tavern and both Genevieve and he sat on the same side, allowing a clear view of the room in front of them.

'So, you think the King is at the centre of this?' the Huntress whispered in his ear just before a barmaid appeared with a sour look on her face.

'What'll you be havin'?'

'Two ales, and two of whatever that roast meat is, thanks.' Culaan answered and the girl sniffed loudly, wiped her nose on her sleeve and cleared the table of the last patron's leftovers before leaving.

'I'm not sure, but it was too easy to get work on his ship and why else would we land in a fishing port? It's not to catch fish, is it?'

'Time will tell.' Genevieve giggled at her own joke. They were getting used to moving through time.

The maid returned with two jugs of ale in one hand and two plates balanced on her other arm. She dropped the jugs so hard they splashed ale onto the stained wooden table before throwing the plates at them, the food sliding to one side on landing.

'That'll be six coppers.' The girl sniffed again. Culaan cursed himself for not changing his coin and pulled out another silver. He was just about to hand it to the girl when Matias arrived.

'I'll fix that up Ruth. You get on with cleaning up this hell hole.' The maid pursed her lips and spoke unpleasant words under her breath as she moved away and the man sat down opposite the Warrior and Huntress.

'You didn't need to do that Tias, but I could do with changing my coin now that you are here. Can you help with that?' Culaan showed his silver coin before placing it back in the draw string bag and returning it inside his vest.

'Of course I can. I'm heartbroken you didn't return to my food stall for your meal,' Matias held his hand to his chest, 'but when I saw you coming into this hovel, I thought I'd do my good Samaritan duty and see to it you came out alive.

'You know we don't need saving Tias. Why are you really here?' Genevieve leant across the table so only the stall holder could hear her.

She pulled her knife from her thigh scabbard for dramatic effect, before using it to cut a chunk of meat, stabbing it and then putting it into her mouth by pulling it from the end of the blade. She followed the food with a long swig of ale as her eyes remained fixed on the man.

Matias swallowed and averted his eyes, then turned to Culaan. 'I heard you got work on the King's ship.' It wasn't a question and Culaan nodded agreement, noting the sudden calm demeanour of their new-found friend. 'Well, there is trouble brewing in town you see.' Matias looked over his shoulder to make sure no one could overhear him.

'Go on.' Culaan coaxed. This was just the information he was looking for. The quicker he completed this mission, the quicker he could be with Ariela.

'Well the King, he's good at killing Catholics.' Culaan nodded even though he had no idea what a Catholic was. 'Well them Catholics are not fond of losing their land or having their priests banished you see.'

Culaan put the pieces together and realised they had fallen into a religious conflict of some sort. 'Matias, why are you telling us this?'

'Well, you aren't from around here, so I'm guessing you don't know the political landscape.' Culaan raised an eyebrow at the rather technical term, suddenly wondering exactly who Matias really was.

'Well then, you've filled us in. Much appreciated.' Culaan filled his mouth and waited, chewing slowly, knowing more was yet to come.

'I'm guessing you don't have a side in this fight yet, so I'm getting in early, before that barbarian leads you astray.'

'The King you mean?' Genevieve grinned as Matias looked over his shoulder once more. She could see the room's occupants were otherwise engaged as a fight broke out amongst two sailors over one whore.

'Huneric is a dangerous son of a bitch and I'm not pulling any punches when I say you should watch your butts, closely.'

'Noted, but that's not the point of this conversation, is it?' Culaan had a pretty good idea where this was leading and it might just be in their favour to play along.

'They, the Catholics that is, are looking for allies.'

'Spies.' Genevieve corrected.

'Yes, yes, whatever you want to call it.' Matias waved his hand. 'They don't call him the Mad King for nothing.'

'You say *they* Tias. What's in it for you? Culaan took a swig of his ale and filled his mouth once more.

Matias studied the two warriors before him carefully, gauging how much he should share. Culaan could see his mind thinking, but didn't push.

'Let's just say I definitely won't be siding with the King anytime soon, but the Catholics might not be any better.'

'So the information you want is for yourself, not the Catholics?' Matias looked at his hands, refusing to make eye contact. Culaan could see he was still deciding what to say and what to keep to himself.

'We aren't mercenaries and we don't fight other people's wars Matias,' Genevieve scoffed but Culaan ignored her and continued, trying not to glare at his sister, 'but we do, let us put it this way, we do stick up for what we think is right.'

Matias nodded and took a deep breath before sighing. 'Let's hope you see the right and wrong of it then. If you hear of anything I should be aware of, you know where to find me.'

Culaan nodded and pulled his pouch from inside his vest, removing five silver coins before placing it back where it came from. 'I trust you Tias. Can you exchange these for me and bring the right coin back?' The Warrior took the man's hand as if to offer a handshake, placing the coins in his palm discreetly.

'I'll be back before you finish your meal.' Matias stood and moved to the bar. He threw some local currency on the counter, which the barmaid scooped up as soon as it touched down.

'That was interesting.' Genevieve stated with a mouthful of meat.

'Very.' Culaan agreed as he lifted his empty jug toward the now all too attentive bar maid.

# Chapter 7

'What do you mean the door was locked?' Ophelia sat on her terrace, a mouthful of dried fruit making it difficult to understand her.

'Exactly what I said. I don't know what's going on Ophelia but I'm not sure the Senator is being entirely honest with us.' Ariela ran her fingers through her wet hair. It felt good to be clean again.

'We are here for a reason. We are going to have to trust that your Angel knows what he is doing. I'm new to all the time travelling, but from what you have told me he seems to want to make sure you succeed.'

Ariela nodded slowly and popped an olive in her mouth. 'I hope Culaan is alright.'

'I'm sure he can look after himself. Genevieve too.' Ophelia spooned some crushed olive paste onto a piece of flat bread and spread it around with the back of the implement. She moaned as the food reached her mouth. 'That is delicious. I could get used to this.' She smiled as she licked the spoon.

There was a knock on Ariela's door followed by Idris entering. The Senator's aid moved toward Ariela and smiled as she saw both young women eating on their balconies. 'Enjoying the food?' she asked as she stepped out to join Ariela.

'Yes, thank you.' Ariela looked over to Ophelia, trying to gauge what they should do next. They needed the Senator to get into the Palace, but what did they need to do once they got there?

'I'm here for your history lesson if you are ready.'

'Can Ophelia come over into my room? It seems silly her sitting only a few steps away on a separate balcony while we discuss this.'

Idris frowned. 'I can't discuss the Order with anyone who isn't ordained.'

'You can't be serious? Ophelia has travelled with me through time. If the Angel thinks she is worthy of the knowledge, then so should you.' Ariela could feel her blood rising.

Who on earth do these people think they are? She is the one who left her family behind. She is the one flipping through time to sort out humanity's atrocities. They have no right to tell her who she can or can't confide in.

'I am just following the Senator's orders Ariela.' Idris's tone was bordering on frustration.

'Then go back to the Senator and tell him I will find my own way into the King's service. If he doesn't trust my judgement, then I'll find someone who does.'

Ariela stood to leave her room. 'Better still. Where is he? I'll tell him myself.'

Idris moved in between the Priestess and the balcony doors, preventing her from leaving the terrace. 'I apologise your Highness. I'm sure it is fine. It just isn't customary.'

'I'd like to leave this room in any case.' Ariela knew now that Idris had to be under orders to keep her in her room, but why?

'I'd rather you didn't. We can bring Ophelia over here, but the Senator has asked that you stay in your room while you are in his estate, at least for now.'

'Is that why I was locked in earlier?' Ariela's nostrils flared as she spoke.

'I had hoped you wouldn't notice.' Idris didn't bat an eye.

'Ariela. Take a breath.' Ophelia was leaning over the balcony railing trying to get as close to her friend as possible. 'I'm sure we can discuss this with the Senator. There is likely a good explanation.'

'Your friend is right. There is a good reason for keeping you here.' Idris indicated the room with her hand.

'What? What reason could there be? The last person who tried to keep me against my will didn't come off so well.' The hair on Ariela's skin began to stand on end as she summoned her powers.

'Princess, please. I am just following orders. The Senator is trying to ensure your introduction to the court is prepared before too many people see you.'

'Why, why would he need to keep me a secret? He already said he was going to introduce me as his niece.'

'Yes, a niece who will also be a suiter to the Prince.'

'No. Absolutely not.' Ariela's hands were tingling now and she knew power was rising to her fingers but the idea of being promised again was proving too much to bear.

'Ariela.' Ophelia climbed over the balcony railing and jumped to her friend's terrace. Idris's eyes grew wide as the woman appeared alongside the Priestess. 'Stop, stop it now. You've never lost control of your powers, don't start now.'

Ariela took a deep breath and closed her eyes. She pictured Culaan holding her in his embrace and the tingling stopped.

'You have to understand Idris, she fled her home to avoid an arranged marriage.' Ophelia looked at the tall woman before her.

'The Senator has no intention of letting a marriage go ahead. He is just laying the bread crumbs to make it easier for Ariela to be close to the King. Prince Hilderic is a gentle soul.

Getting close to him will be safe and allow you easy access to the King.'

Ariela took another deep breath and opened her eyes. 'I'm sorry. When I discovered my door was locked, I grew suspicious, but when you said an arranged marriage, after what the Senator was going on about earlier, I just assumed he believed marrying me off would stop the religious turmoil.'

'Nothing of the sort.' Idris looked at Ophelia and smiled. 'Well your friend is here now in any case, so let us start your history lesson.'

****

Hearing how her mother and father died wasn't easy, but she was relieved to know she had not left them without any knowledge of where she was going or what she was doing.

Idris explained how the Priestess Order of Shiloh had continued to grow over the centuries and that the Order now flourished throughout Europe and Asia. Young women who had no place else to go were chosen to join the Order. They were trained to fight and if they possessed gifts, they were encouraged and tutored in how to use them.

Idris was a fighter as Ariela had suspected. She possessed no special gifts that she knew of and had served the Order after being accepted as an orphan. Her parents were killed by the King and her family's wealth stolen.

'Did you believe her?' Ophelia sat on Ariela's bed and looked at the closed door after Idris left.

Ariela bit her lip. 'About the Christ child, the Order… yes. About why I was locked in my room, I don't think so, but maybe she doesn't really know why. She is just doing as she is told.'

'I think you might be right. Do we sit here and wait on the Senator or find out for ourselves?' Ophelia grinned mischievously and Ariela giggled.

'They don't know I can travel in this realm. I think I might do a little snooping around.'

'That's not fair.' Ophelia pouted and flung herself onto the bed. 'I can't follow you if you do that.'

'True. Do you think they have locked the door again?' Ariela stood up and moved to the door, Ophelia shuffling on the bed, preparing to follow. She turned the knob and smiled as it moved freely. She opened it a crack and peered out.

Two tall women with long braids and short tunics looked over their shoulder at the sound. Ariela opened the door fully, not wanting to appear to be tentative.

'Can we get something for you?' the red-haired woman asked, bowing respectfully.

'No thank you, just going for a walk.' Ariela moved out to test just how freely she was going to be able to move around.

'Sorry.' Both women moved toward the door. 'The Senator has asked that you stay in your room until preparations have been made.

Ariela smiled and resisted the urged to use her powers. 'You don't mind if my friend stays with me for a while though?'

The two guards looked at each other and then nodded to the Priestess. She smiled and returned to her room.

'If they knock, I'm on the balcony. Just keep them out until I get back. I'm going to find out why we are under guard and if Titus knows anything about this.'

Ophelia nodded and laid back down on the bed as a swirl of air moved around Ariela and she disappeared.

Chapter 8

'My goodness.' Martha jumped as the Priestess opened the door to the store room into the tavern. 'You frightened me half to death.'

Ariela smiled and patted the older woman on the shoulder. 'Where is Titus? I need to speak with him.'

'How did you get here?' Martha frowned, looking over Ariela's shoulder, trying to see if anyone else was with her.

'Titus, is he here?' Ariela wondered why everyone was so secretive, but dismissed her frustrations. The Order needed to stay protected and it must have been very difficult to stay hidden in plain sight as they did.

'I will fetch him for you.' Martha wiped her hands on her apron, white splashes of flour stained the fabric.

A few moments later, Titus walked through the doorway. 'Ariela, I didn't expect you to be returning. Does the Senator know you are here? How did you get here?'

'I have a few questions Titus. Why has the Senator locked me in my room?'

Titus took a sharp breath. 'I have no idea your Highness, you must believe me.'

Ariela studied the man's face. She had no reason to think he was lying, but if he was the Senator's man, she needed to be careful.

'How did you get here if you were locked in your room?' Titus' manner seemed a little agitated.

'I climbed out my window.' Ariela smiled as Titus raised an eyebrow, but remained silent a moment.

'I'll arrange for a carriage to take you home now.' Titus turned and moved toward the door.

'That won't be necessary Titus. I found my own way here; I will find my own way back. Are you sure you can't tell me more?'

Titus looked over his shoulder. Martha was too far away to hear, but he only shrugged. If he knew anything, he wasn't sharing it.

Ariela sighed and opened the storeroom door and made her way back to the tunnel. She prepared to travel back to the estate, but instead of going to her room, she decided to find out more about what the Senator was up to.

She did not know her way around the Senator's estate. So far, she had only seen the courtyard, the grand staircase and the hallway leading to their rooms.

She was unsure if she should arrive in the courtyard, it could be full of Priestesses, staff or the Senator himself.

Ariela had travelled to unknown places before, it was just far more difficult than going to a place she knew. She took a deep breath and focussed on the energy around her. The dark tunnel disappeared as Ariela found her way to the cookhouse. The smell of food always made it easier to find.

She ducked into a dark corner as soon as she arrived and listened carefully for voices or noise of anyone moving. She heard the cook yelling at one of his staff and the smell of cooking fish hung in the air. It was past midday and the staff would be working to prepare the evening meal.

Instead of moving toward the cookhouse, she moved away, down a stone corridor that grew darker with each step. Voices drifted to her ears and she listened carefully, trying to work out where they were coming from.

She could hear two men arguing. The voices came from above her head, in the next floor up. The wooden floor creaked as one of the men paced the room from one side to the other.

She wanted to move closer but she wasn't sure where to go. She needed to find stairs. The Priestess followed the corridor until she reached the end. Ariela frowned and turned around in a complete circle to take in her surroundings. The hallway had gone on for thirty or more paces with no doors, no stairs and no obvious reason for its existence.

'Why on earth have a hallway to no-where?' She knew that didn't make sense. The Priestess moved back along the hallway until she felt a breeze moving past her feet. She stopped and touched the thick stone wall, placing her cheek and ear against it to listen for any movement.

She searched the rough surface for a hand-hold, a lever or anything that might open the door she knew must be there, but nothing. It was well disguised. Someone didn't want this room to be found.

With no obvious way in, Ariela decided she could jump into the space behind the wall. It was a risk. If the room didn't exist, she could be trapped in the stone. She composed herself and leapt the short distance, opening her eyes into complete darkness. At least she was alone.

The Priestess pulled on her power and formed a small ball of light in the palm of her hand. She held the light out and slowly circled the room. There were walls of wooden shelves, filled with old scrolls, all stacked neatly and catalogued with the year marked on the shelf.

A metal staircase stood in the corner, leading up to the floor Ariela wanted to get to, but the sound of the voices told her she would open a door right in their midst—something she didn't want to do.

Instead, she moved to the spiral staircase, reaching out to touch the cold railing and placing her foot on the first step. She took a slow, deep breath as she moved to the next, praying it wouldn't creak. The closer she got to the hidden door, the easier she could hear the voices.

One was the Senator's, but the other man she did not recognise.

'She has accepted our story. The Priestess will infiltrate the King's court and be our eyes and ears.' Ariela recognised the Senator's words.

'And she doesn't know I'm involved?' the unknown man asked.

'No. I've kept her in her room until you leave tonight. Don't return until I send word.'

'Do you really believe she'll kill the King on your say so?'

'She has been trained to kill. The Order does nothing, if not train these young women to kill for God's glory with fanatical zeal.'

Ariela gasped at the Senator's words. These poor girls were being used by politicians and they had no idea. She moved back down the stairs to see if she could discover more about her family. She doubted what Idris told her was the whole truth judging by what she had just heard. Maybe the scrolls could reveal more about the Order or her parents.

As she moved to the final step, she tripped and cursed as she landed on the dirt floor heavily. The voices above her stopped suddenly as she scrambled for a dark corner.

The sound of feet moving quickly on the wooden floor made her push herself into the stone wall, hoping to disappear in the darkness. Light streamed down the metal stairs as the door flung open. Ariela observed it was a trap door which must have been hidden in the Senator's study. *More secrets.*

A man looked down to the room below. 'Who is there? Show yourself.' The Senator barked.

Ariela had no choice. She couldn't be discovered in the hidden room. Instead of getting to look through the scrolls, she would have to return to her room. The air around her shimmered and she disappeared as the Senator began his descent into the hidden library.

****

'Can you see anything?' The Senator's visitor called from above.

'No. There is no one down here. It was probably a rat.' The Senator shone his lamp over the hard-packed dirt and a footprint caught his eye. 'A very big rat.' He whispered. 'One that doesn't need to open secret doors.'

# Chapter 9

Culaan followed Genevieve onto the ship, watching carefully as the crew cast their eye her way. He couldn't explain it exactly, but since discovering she was his sister, he had become somehow more protective of her. He knew she could look after herself, but he felt responsible like he never had before.

'There was a time when I would have been overjoyed at you watching my butt like that, but you are going to have to relax brother.' Genevieve looked over her shoulder and winked at Culaan before stepping over the railing and onto the ship.

Hoots and hollers followed her as she strolled along the deck and up the stairs to the helm. She bowed for the men as Culaan guarded the stairs, his arms across his chest, suddenly wondering if bringing Genevieve on board was such a good idea.

'Thank you, thank you.' Genevieve smiled. 'Such a warm welcome.' One man with a missing front tooth moved forward, pushing his way past Culaan as more men flooded toward the Huntress.

Culaan moved to draw his sword, but Genevieve shook her head and waved her finger at her brother. His chest heaved with rage, but he knew better than to move if his sister didn't want him to.

The toothless man reached Genevieve first and she thumped him in the nose with her fist. The audible crack made Culaan wince and feel slightly sorry for the man.

'She broke my nose!' he screamed through his hands as blood spilled to the worn wooden deck below his feet.

'Look, but don't touch little man. That's the rule.' Genevieve held her hand up in front of her, palm facing the sailor and waving back and forth.

'You bitch.' The man stormed forward as his friends began to slow their advance.

Genevieve ducked and used the man's momentum to send him over the railing, arms and legs flailing as he fell to the deck below the Captain's helm. There was a sudden silence that followed the thud of the sailor hitting the deck. Then the hoots and laughter erupted and the sailor was lifted to his feet by his crewmates, unconscious and oblivious to the amusement he had invoked.

'I see you have already introduced yourself.' The Captain moved from his cabin to the Huntress and surveyed the blood smear on the deck below.

Genevieve shrugged. 'We aren't exactly on a first name basis yet, but getting there.' She smiled and the Captain returned the gesture, the scars on his face pulling with the motion.

The Huntress resisted the urge to lick her lips. He really was quite gorgeous.

Culaan moved alongside, looking from Genevieve to the Captain and back again, a big grin on his face. 'I hope I'm not interrupting anything but I think that's the King arriving now.'

A tall black stallion pranced up the wharf, with a group of soldiers all dressed in black leather armour, trotting on foot alongside.

'That's the Kings Guard,' the Captain offered, not taking his eyes from the Huntress.

'Do we get that armour? I'll look fabulous in that outfit.' She smiled as the Captain raised an eyebrow.

'You do. I sent word that I'd found new recruits, but I doubt the armour will fit as well as you hope. It's not exactly made to suit your body shape.'

'True.' Genevieve nodded as she sulked.

'Do we need to finish giving our instructions to the crew?' Culaan asked as the King dismounted and his guard fanned out to create a perimeter for his protection while he climbed aboard.

'I think Genevieve has made her point. I can't see the men bothering her again, but just to be safe, take different watches for the first night.'

Culaan nodded his understanding. If they were both asleep, the men might get the jump on both of them, but with one of them always awake, that was less likely.

The King was taller than Culaan by half a head and the Warrior watched him carefully as he walked up the gangplank. He was a fighting man with good balance, posture and obvious strength.

'Your Grace.' The Captain bowed deeply, Culaan and Genevieve followed.

'Are these the two warriors you spoke of?' The King's voice was deep and carried an unwavering authority - the confidence of a man born to rule.

'Yes your Grace. Let me introduce Genevieve and Culaan. Brother and sister warriors.'

The King studied Culaan carefully from top to toe and almost grunted his approval. 'You will do.' Culaan bit back the retort on his tongue and frowned at Genevieve's smile.

The King turned to Genevieve and touched her cheek. The Huntress moved away from his hand slowly and smirked in a less than friendly manner. 'Now you my dear are too beautiful to be a warrior. I have other uses for you.'

'I assure you that would not be wise.' The Huntress spoke barely above a whisper and the King's eyebrows both rose at her words.

'I'm not accustomed to refusal woman,' the King snarled.

'Oh, sorry my Lord. I didn't realise I had refused anything. You misunderstand, it's just that I'm a trained warrior and I've been known to wake up with terrible nightmares and well, let's say I've maimed and killed a few lovers over the years.'

The Captain fought hard not to laugh and coughed to cover his failure.

The King looked at the Captain and frowned. 'I hired her for a reason your Grace,' he tried to clarify. 'She is an excellent shot with that bow.' The Captain nodded and Genevieve drew and shot, taking the fire stick from the lantern lighter's hand on the far side of the ship, pinning the lantern he had been holding to the wooden wall in the process.

'I see.' The King turned on his heel and moved toward the Captain's chambers.

As he disappeared, Genevieve leant in closely. 'Thanks for the support. Does he usually take your bed when he's on board?'

'Of course. It's his ship.'

'So you are employed?' Culaan joined the conversation.

'I am, not by choice but through necessity.'

'This was your ship,' Genevieve stated.

'It was. The King is formidable and ruthless.' The Captain did not continue his explanation. Instead, his eyes grew distant, as if remembering something best forgotten. Genevieve knew that look and touched the man's arm.

'Where do we sleep?' she smiled.

'On deck, with the rest of the King's men.' The Captain welcomed the distraction. 'I'll introduce you to the Captain of the guard and he'll see to it you get the armour you need.' The Captain nodded to the man with a broad chest and a scar on his cheek. It ran through his eye, all the way down to the corner of his mouth, giving him a permanent, unfriendly sneer.

'That's a face only a mother can love.' Genevieve spoke from the corner of her mouth, not turning her head away from the scarred warrior.

'He is as ruthless as he looks. Watch your step with Roderic. His ambition rivals that of the King himself.'

# Chapter 10

Ophelia almost fell off the bed as Ariela arrived out of thin air. She clasped her chest with her hand. 'I'll never get used to that.'

'Our Senator has a visitor he doesn't want us to know about, which is why he's been keeping us locked up.'

'That makes sense. Who is the visitor?'

'I couldn't discover who he was, but the Senator is conspiring to have me kill the King. He's been using the Order for political gain.'

Ophelia was intrigued and crossed her legs on the bed, facing Ariela. 'How so?'

'I'm not exactly sure. He said something about how the girls were trained to take orders and kill whoever they were told to, in the defence of their God.'

'Oh, but whose god? Yours or his?'

'I barely understand any of this new religion, but I think it's the same god. He told us himself the Christ child is born of my line, the line of my Uncle David, an Israelite.'

'Well we don't do anyone's bidding, do we?' Ophelia looked to her friend for confirmation.

'I have no idea to be honest Ophelia. I've been doing Raziel's bidding or God's bidding so I thought. Maybe I am being used afterall?'

'No.' Ophelia jumped to her feet and embraced Ariela. 'You do what you believe is right, not what anyone else tells you to do. You fight evil. You don't choose political or religious sides or follow anyone's agenda.'

'I've got to be following something. What is it?' Ariela couldn't decide if she was angry or on the verge of tears.

'A feeling. The feeling you are doing the right thing. You say you can hear the Angel talk to you. Do you really believe he wouldn't lead you in the right direction? These men aren't led by an angel. They are led by ego. You don't know men like I know men Ariela.'

Ariela moved away from her friend and opened her bag of artefacts that still sat on her bed. The sun was setting and she didn't want to leave them in plain sight any longer.

'You're right. I don't know men very well and the few I've met so far, except for Culaan, have been driven by delusions of grandeur. I get it. That must be why God put my mother in charge of the Shiloh Order.' The Priestess giggled and Ophelia joined her.

'What are you doing with those?' Ophelia asked as the Priestess took inventory of all the artefacts they had collected so far. She held her mother's amulet in her hands and clutched it to her chest. It glowed as she wrapped her hands around it.

'I'm going to hide them.'

'Where?' Ophelia looked around the room. 'You can't leave them here.'

'I won't. I'm going to hide them in a place one of my closest friends once told me about.'

'What friend?'

'When I was young and alone in the Shiloh fortress, I didn't have many friends. All the Priestesses saw me as special, someone they couldn't get too close to because of who I was. My father did most of my training, but there were a few others. My aunt who was a very powerful Priestess, my Uncle who was the General of the King's army and a little holy man from a foreign land. His name was Narayana. I really miss him.'

'Narayana? Holy man?'

'Yes. He had tricks he could do. They were magic really or gifts, depending on whom you believe gives us the talents we have. Narayana could move through space in a similar way to how I do but he could also make holes, to hide things in.'

Ophelia was listening intently, her mouth open as wide as her eyes.

Ariela had a distant view in her eyes as she spoke. 'Narayana carried a bag over his shoulder that he could reach into from anywhere and get out anything he had hidden in that special hole in space. What I don't know yet is if it will work when we jump through time and I'm not willing to leave these behind.' Ariela lifted the bag as she spoke.

'But you can use it to keep them safe in this time.' Ophelia was excited by the idea.

'Yes. I'll show you.' Ariela took the bag and placed the artefacts back inside. She laid it on the bed and the bed swallowed the bag like an ocean of water.

'Oh my goodness. Where did it go?'

'Here.' Ariela reached into the golden coloured bedspread and pulled the bag back out. 'I just need to keep the bag and send the objects. I've never done more than a single solid item at one time.'

'Oh. You'll get it. Just keep practising. We have plenty of time.' Ophelia laughed. 'We are stuck in here after all.' She waved her hand around the large room.

'True.' Ariela collected the objects on top of the bag and tried to push them into the Void, but there was no way of keeping the bag and the items separate using this method.

She put the artefacts back in the bag and then placed the bag over her shoulder. This was how she had seen Narayana collect his items on so many occasions. She put her hand in the bag and tried to push all the items into the Void at once. It didn't work, her hand just wasn't big enough.

She suddenly realised her mistake. Instead of pushing all the artefacts into the Void at once, she meticulously took each item, one at a time and placed them into the Void, the world between, well she didn't really know what the Void was between but she placed the artefacts through the bag and into the hiding place she had selected.

The Priestess put her hand back into the empty bag and reached for one item, pulling out Brísingamen, the artefact that helped her transfer Culaan's powers to him from his mother.

'It worked. I can't believe you did it.' Ophelia was jumping up and down.

'Thanks for the vote of confidence.'

'Well, you know what I mean. That is so amazing. It would be great if we could make it work through time. How can we test that?'

Ariela thought about it a moment and then she suddenly laughed. 'I can't believe I didn't think of it earlier. I'll just make another spot before we leave and put something worthless in it. If I can reach it when we arrive in the next time, then I'll be able to put the artefacts in the Void after that.'

'That is clever.' A knock on the door interrupted their excitement. The girls looked out the door to the balcony with the beautiful sea view and suddenly realised the sun had set.

'Come in,' Ariela called and Idris opened the door and smiled at the cheerful grins of both girls as they sat on the bed, the seemingly empty bag on the covers behind them.

'The Senator has made the arrangements and you are free to look around his estate now. The servants are all briefed and the Senator will see you at dinner shortly.'

'How will we find the dining room?' Ophelia asked.

'If you haven't stumbled on it by accident, then I'll come and find you. Just one thing, if you find a locked room, please don't try and enter. There are some private chambers in the estate.'

'Of course.' Ariela smiled innocently and Ophelia struggled not to snigger. 'Idris, do you like being a part of the Order?'

Idris tried to hide her shock. She had been in her fourth year when her parents were killed by the King. She barely remembered her mother's face and the Order is all she had ever really known.

'I enjoy the training. I love the other Priestesses like my own sisters, although I don't see as many of them as I used to, now that I work with the Senator.'

'Have you ever killed for the Order?' Ariela considered if she should push this line of questioning, but she needed to know just how the Priestesses were exploited for political advantage.

Idris was old enough to have seen battle if there had been any. She bore no obvious scars, so Ariela only hoped she hadn't been asked to murder someone like she now knew she would be.

'I've not, but I know a few who have. The survival of the Order is paramount. Your Mother's teachings say just so.'

Ariela raised an eyebrow. 'Where are these teachings?'

'They are not written; they are passed down by those who lead us.'

'Oh. Interesting.'

'Interesting?' Idris had an edge to her voice as she questioned the Priestess.

'It's probably nothing, but,' Ariela scratched the back of her neck for added effect, 'that doesn't sound like something my mother would have said.'

She did not stay to see the reaction on the Priestess' face, instead she grabbed Ophelia by the hand and skipped from the room like a little girl going to fetch flowers in the fields.

Chapter 11

The sun rose over the ocean as the ship made its way toward Malta. There wasn't a cloud in the sky or a breath of wind, so the oars were in full swing.

'You're lucky it isn't rough. I've heard they can get waves that break over the bow of this big girl.' Culaan smiled as Genevieve hurled the remainder of her stomach contents over the side of the ship.

She looked up, throwing her long plait over her shoulder and scowled. A moan left her lips involuntarily as she swatted away Culaan's unexpected sympathetic pat on her back.

'Maybe being a guard on the King's ship isn't such a great idea after all.'

'You think!' Genevieve almost growled. 'I need some water.' She staggered away from the railing, only to rush back for another shot at hurling into the waters.

'You stay here. I'll get your water.' Culaan tapped her shoulder as he left the side of the ship.

'You'll be glad when we make shore by the look of you.' The Captain tried unsuccessfully not to grin.

'Aren't you supposed to be steering this thing?' Genevieve didn't take her eyes from the water below.

'Even a Captain needs a break.' There was a long silence as the Captain considered his words carefully.

'You're obviously a great fighter, but serving on this vessel isn't going to work out in the long run for you. You are going to have to find work on Malta or another passage back to Carthage. I'm sorry.'

Genevieve shrugged. She knew they needed to be near the King but she had no intention of staying on-board the ship. 'We'll figure something out.'

The Captain nodded and continued his inspection before returning to the helm. Culaan appeared with her water a moment later, which she drank greedily.

'Slow down. You'll just throw it back up otherwise.' He held the wooden ladle of water and forced his sister to drink slowly. 'What did the Captain want?'

'Oh. Just letting us know we're fired.'

****

The port was teeming with traders on the dawn of their second day aboard. Genevieve was starving, as she staggered from the ship to the jeers of the sailors on-board. Her face was still pale, but her spirits lifted the moment her feet touched the land once more.

She resisted the temptation to drop to her knees and kiss the solid ground.

'I need food.' Genevieve staggered like a drunken sailor, but Culaan held her up, placing his arm around her waist for support.

'Do you think you can keep it down?'

'Now that the ship isn't lurching my stomach around like a stone in a sling, yes.'

'We need to find another way to get into the King's employ once more. I might have an idea, but we need to get you back to full strength first.'

Genevieve frowned at Culaan's enthusiasm. 'I'm not sure being in his employ is such a good idea. You saw the way he looked at me and he's a man used to getting what he wants.'

'Don't worry. You'll be far too valuable to him to bother with bedding you after what I have in mind. While you were ….' Culaan searched for the right word, 'otherwise occupied, I listened in on a few of the crew's conversations. It seems our good King, and I use that term loosely, has a habit of causing conflict here.'

The pair pushed through a crowded marketplace set up along the docks. Conversation was limited, so they stopped at a food stall and Culaan passed a couple of coins to the short, lean young merchant in exchange for rolled flatbread filled with freshly cooked meat and goats' cheese, dripping with a sauce he couldn't quite make out.

'No surprises there.' Genevieve scoffed through a mouthful of food. She sighed as she took her first mouthful. 'This is delicious.'

Culaan nodded and tried to study the contents, but Genevieve nudged him to continue his conversation.

'He has been raiding the Catholic's that Matias was talking about here too. Apparently, they have quite a lot of wealth and King Huneric likes to take it away from them. Some religious feud or something.'

The Warrior nodded toward a quiet alley and the pair moved away from the crowd and down the narrow walkway, barely wide enough for the two of them to walk side by side.

The stone buildings shaded the alley from the rising sun, but it was light enough to see where they were going. The only problem was, they had no idea where they were heading.

'So, what is the plan?' Genevieve asked just before she stuffed the last mouthful of food in her mouth, suddenly realising that she might not have left enough room to chew.

Culaan smiled as his sister's cheeks expanded but knew better than to say anything. She had a habit of thumping him in the arm if he teased her.

'I say we defend them.'

'Who?' Genevieve spoke over her still full mouth.

'The Catholics.'

'Won't that make us the King's enemy?' The huntress tried to swallow her mouthful and decided more chewing was in order.

Culaan shook his head. 'That's the best bit about being a mercenary. He'll ask us what they are paying and he'll offer more. I guarantee it.'

Genevieve looked dubious. 'First we have to beat him.'

'Yes, and we have to do it without revealing our powers. We will likely need them to remain our little secret until we really need them.'

Chapter 12

'Hold still Ariela, I need to tighten this up more.' Idris pulled roughly on the laces that tied the back of Ariela's dress.

'How on earth is anyone supposed to breathe with all this?' She held up the heavy tunic that Idris had just placed over her head and frowned as she tied a long sash around her waist.

'This is ridiculous. I'm going to suffocate under all this fabric and how can I eat with this tied so tightly?' The Priestess tried to loosen the wide band of fabric with her thumbs.

'Eat? My dear, you peck at your food, you don't eat in the company of men.' Idris suppressed a giggle as she draped the long sash over Ariela's shoulder.

'It's like my Uncle's court all over again. Stay in the corner and don't let anyone know you have a brain or a single solitary independent thought. I've travelled through centuries and thought surely these tired old ideas would have died out by now.'

'Not at all. The world is still run by men Ariela.' Idris fussed with the Priestess's hair.

'So it would seem.'

Idris dragged her over to a tall bronze mirror and Ariela stopped mid-sentence. The dress was a cream colour, partially covered by an emerald green tunic edged with golden bands of intricately embroidered patterns. Her waist was wrapped in a soft, sheer material that draped over her shoulder and hung to the ground with a long trailing grand occasions train.

Her hair had been braided and tied up on top of her head like a beehive, with golden ribbons intricately laced through it.

'Do I really have to get this dressed up every time I go to the King's court?'

'I'm afraid so. It's a full day event, just to appear.' Idris opened the door and Ariela attempted to make her way through. The long trailing hem of her dress caught and nearly pulled her from her feet.

'You'll get used to it, but you need to lift the fabric over your arm as you are going through narrow doorways and up or down stairs.'

Idris draped the fabric over Ariela's arm as she studied the doorway. It wasn't narrow. She and Culaan could easily walk through side by side if they were wearing *normal* clothing.

Idris knocked on Ophelia's doors. The former Keeper had a smile from ear to ear as she pranced out the door of her room.

'Isn't this gorgeous!' Ophelia lifted the deep wine-red fabric in her hand and twirled like a dancer. 'I never thought I'd ever wear something this beautiful.'

'You're actually enjoying all this pomp and ceremony?' Ariela rolled her eyes.

'Oh just relax and try to enjoy it too Ariela.'

'You know we aren't supposed to eat in these things.' The Priestess lifted the fabric of her own dress with disdain. 'I'm going to starve.'

'We can scoff ourselves silly after the men withdraw. It's customary in any case. I'll undo your laces, you can undo mine and we'll raid the cookhouse before we come back to the Senator's estate.'

Ariela wasn't convinced but she followed her friend to the carriage which awaited them in the Senator's courtyard.

'Is the Senator joining us?' Ariela asked Idris as the footmen opened the door to the carriage.

'He is already there.' Idris advised. 'He'll meet the carriage and introduce you. I know this is a mission, but try to enjoy it where you can.' Idris held Ariela's hand affectionately, as a bigger sister would her younger.

The girls were slowly mastering staying in their seats as the carriage lurched and bounced along the rough stone roadways.

'Why not just leave the road hard-packed dirt? Why all the fancy stones? I'm sure they put them there to slow the carriages down. Give me a standing chariot any day.' Ariela continued to grumble until the carriage made an abrupt stop.

The door swung open and the pale hand of the Senator reached in to offer them assistance.

'Ariela, Ophelia, it is time for your introduction to the King's court. Now remember what Idris has taught you. You must keep your manners in place at all times.'

'I might look like a child Senator, but I've seen a lot in a very short time. I think we'll be just fine.' Ariela spoke quietly as the Senator took her hand. The man smiled knowingly and followed them up the stairs and into the palace courtyard.

The steps were marble, the courtyard was marble, the statues were marble. Ariela had never seen so much gleaming stone in her life. The temple they had seen on their first day was not a patch on the King's palace. The walls were bright sandstone, and the courtyard walls were higher than the Priestess thought possible to build.

'Spectacular isn't it,' the Senator spoke as he joined the girls. 'Here, take my arm. 'He placed both his hands on his hips and Ophelia looped her arm through. Ariela shrugged and did the same on the other side.

The music floated on the afternoon breeze and the aroma of cooked food and summer fruits made Ariela's stomach growl. 'I should have eaten before we came.'

The doormen opened two large dark wooden doors. They were carved with swirling patterns, the tops cut right through to allow the breeze to circulate. It was little help to Ariela, her back was damp with perspiration and she could feel the drips of moisture under her breasts.

'If I faint, I'm sorry but I think these dresses were created as someone's warped idea of female torture.'

Ophelia giggled but brought her hand to her lips as Idris had instructed.

'That's right Ophelia, don't show those teeth in public.' Ariela seethed and the Senator had given up on stern looks, instead his eyes were pleading.

The Priestess rolled her eyes one last time as they moved through the massive entrance and into the hall beyond.

Couples danced to the music, a full arm's width apart. The colourful skirts of all the fancy dresses swirled and flew around like they were floating on air.

Even Ariela had to admit, it was an amazing sight. A tall young man, around Culaan's age stepped forward to greet the Senator.

'I am sorry Senator, but my father could not be here today. He is in Malta, attending to…business.' The young man stammered slightly and looked at the floor, seemingly embarrassed.

'Hilderic. That is to be expected. Please, I'd like to introduce my niece Ariela and her closest friend Ophelia.' The young man took Ariela's hand and kissed the back of it lightly with his lips. His eyes were friendly and warm and the Priestess found herself returning his genuine smile.

'Ladies. This is Prince Hilderic, son of the King.' The Senator stepped back. 'I hope you won't mind showing my niece around, your highness. If your father is not here, I do have a few dignitaries I should be catching up with.'

'Not at all Senator. It would be my pleasure.' A piece of blonde hair fell from the Prince's ponytail as he nodded and the Senator bowed before moving away.

'That was some brush off.' Ariela spoke before thinking the comment through. The Prince laughed good-naturedly.

'I'm quite used to it Ariela.'

'Why?' Ophelia jabbed her in the ribs and she quickly added. 'If you don't mind me asking of course your Highness.'

'Not at all.' The Prince assumed the arm position the Senator had previously adopted and both girls linked arms with him. 'I'm Huneric's son, but I'm not known to have his, shall we say, *charisma*. I'm also not next in line for the throne, that's my cousin's place. So, you see, I'm no further up the food chain than the Senator or most of the dignitaries he has gone to rub shoulders with. In fact, I'm likely to be further down the line of influence than most of them.'

'That's not really the point. You're still the King's son.' Hilderic studied the Priestess a moment, as though he were trying to put pieces of a puzzle together.

'Where did you say you were from?'

'I didn't.' Ariela stopped asking questions, suddenly realising she must have said too much already.

'Where can we find a drink your highness?' Ophelia asked, hoping to distract the Prince.

The prince smiled knowingly. 'Please, call me Hilderic. As I said, my title isn't important. I'll take you to the buffet. We should be able to find you a glass of wine or fruit juice.'

Definitely fruit juice Ariela told herself. She needed to look and listen more and speak a lot less.

Ariela's stomach growled again as she passed the buffet and the Prince chuckled. 'You haven't been to many of these functions have you.' It wasn't a question.

'My uncle decided I needed some grooming.' Ariela started to tell the tale as planned. 'Court isn't exactly part of our everyday life. That's why Ophelia is with me, for moral support.'

'The Prince looked around and studied the faces beyond the buffet. Look, unless you are enjoying all this fanfare, I'm happy to take you both someplace where you can relax a little more openly.'

Ariela grinned as Ophelia shook her head. 'What? The Sen, Uncle won't mind. I'm just being polite with the Prince. I'm sure he wouldn't want me to be impolite and refuse such a *generous* offer.'

Ophelia feigned an objection, but Ariela was already nodding. 'Let's go. I'm sure I can ease into this new lifestyle with a little bit of help. Lead the way Hilderic.'

Chapter 13

The Priest was unconscious, a large gash in his forehead spilling blood to the stone covered ground. Smoke rose through the broken round stained-glass window below the small belltower that framed the doorway.

Culaan had planned to intervene for tactical reasons, but as the Priest lay unconscious, the King's guard continued to kick and thump him.

'Well?' Genevieve asked, waiting on her brother to enact his plan.

'Draw and shoot only the two closest to the Priest Then follow my lead but stay hidden for now.'

Genevieve nodded and notched an arrow. The first man fell as the next arrow struck its mark on the second. The commotion was short lived—these were well trained soldiers of the King's personal guard.

Culaan moved from their hiding place, his sword drawn. He casually rolled it around his wrist, moving forward leaving Genevieve a clear line of fire.

'What is the meaning of this?' the King demanded, still seated comfortably on his horse, not bothering to join the fray.

'Just a little intervention your Highness.'

'But you work for *me*!'

'We were let go on arriving. You see my sister's stomach doesn't seem to enjoy sailing as we had hoped. Your Captain gave us our marching orders so we had to find alternative work.' Culaan pointed his sword to the still unconscious Priest.

'How can he pay you if he's dead?' The King dismounted, undeterred by Culaan's drawn weapon.

'He doesn't. Let us just say he seems to have a benefactor willing to pay handsomely.'

'You'll earn every coin of that payment before I'm finished with you boy.' The King dismounted and drew his own weapon, moving toward Culaan, three remaining guards at his side. The man was no coward it seemed and the glint in his eye was manic.

Culaan felt a strange pulse of energy from the King, something his mother's magic must been interpreting. An arrow flew past Culaan taking the soldier on the King's right, in the eye. The man crumpled to the ground as the King charged.

Culaan's sword connected with the King's with a hum that both warriors felt. The King raised an eyebrow. 'Whatever they are paying you, I'll double it.'

Culaan didn't reply. Genevieve shouldered her bow, the close fighting rendering it useless. She drew her sword and moved to join her brother.

The remaining two guards on the King's left noticed the Huntress and moved to intercept her. Culaan's blade continued to pulse and he fought to keep from revealing his power. It was as though the blade could sense something in the King and it wanted to fight what it could feel. It took all his strength and concentration to keep the light from igniting.

'Who is paying you?' The King moved back to give himself room to swing. Culaan followed, not wanting to open the space between them.

'What makes you think we can be bought?' Culaan gauged how long he needed to hold out. A mercenary had no personal stake in any fight. He needed to keep his emotions in check.

'All mercenaries can be bought.'

'We have a job to finish. It's all about reputation. You understand.' Culaan didn't want to see the Priest die so that he could bring his plan to fruition, but he also knew he had to step down from this fight to earn the King's trust.

'A dilemma. I can see.' The King's sword connected with Culaan's again and both men circled, locked together, neither wanting to open the gap to allow the other the advantage.

'The Priest lives… we take the spoils. I'm sure you can sell that to your employer.' Culaan stepped back this time, but the King followed him, unsure if he had made his point or not.

Genevieve elbowed one opponent in the head and stepped back. The second moved into the gap as the Huntress swung her sword, taking the soldier in the neck. The man's eyes grew wide as the wound began to bubble with blood. He dropped his weapon and fought to stem the bleeding, but within seconds, he had collapsed to the ground.

The second soldier was more wary, circling Genevieve from a distance. The Huntress smiled contemptuously and casually lowered her weapon, trying to goad him into a rash attack.

The man remained cautious. 'We can do this all day sweetheart.' Genevieve tried again to get behind the man's guard.

He snorted and moved in to Genevieve's weak side. She resisted the urge to send a wave of power to unbalance him. This fight had to be won without magic. She tossed her weapon into her left hand and met the man's sword with her own. Pulling her dagger from her thigh scabbard, she thrust the weapon under the soldier's left armpit, finding soft, unprotected flesh.

The last King's guard fell with a look of bewilderment in his eyes.

'It seems we have the advantage, so let's renegotiate, shall we?' Culaan smiled and the King took in a slow and ragged breath, his anger evident in his eyes.

'You are both formidable fighters, that is obvious and if you were zealots from that damned Catholic cause I'd be dead already, so whatever your terms, I'll agree.' The King moved back and sheathed his sword.

Genevieve wiped her dagger clean on the dead man's tunic but did not sheath her weapons. Culaan nodded to her and she shrugged before putting her dagger away and sheathing her sword. He then did the same.

'The Priest goes free and the spoils stay. We were tasked with saving both. You pay us double what we were offered, and then three silver coins a day each for as long as we are in your employ.'

'I'm hardly able to negotiate from this position, but that seems fair considering your expertise. However, I might need more specialised services from time to time. I'll reward you handsomely of course.'

Culaan didn't like the sound of it, but he shrugged casually. 'As long as it doesn't involve sleeping with my sister, then we'll assess the merits when the time comes.'

The King nodded and moved to his horse. 'Be back at the ship before nightfall. We leave port before sunset, then we'll talk about who the traitor was who employed you to save this Catholic wretch and we'll also discuss your roles.'

Culaan nodded as the King's horse trotted away from the burnt out little stone church. 'Oh, and get this mess cleaned up,' the King called without a backward glance.

'That was too easy.' Genevieve commented as the Priest began to stir.

'No, he sensed my power, I know it.'

'What, your sword didn't light up. There were no pulses of air, how?'

'Our swords buzzed like bees when they touched. He's got some sort of power of his own Genie and keeping me close is the only reason my foolhardy plan worked.'

A noise from the ground drew their attention. The Priest grunted as he rolled onto all fours, trying to regain his feet. He clutched his side and winced. 'What happened?' he asked as Genevieve helped him to stand.

'The King raided your church, but we managed to stop him before they killed you. Was there anyone else here?' Genevieve asked, helping the Priest to take a seat on the stone wall that surrounded the church. Flowering creepers cascaded down the side, belying the smoke and destruction that spilled from within.

'No one else. Just me.'

'Why did he raid the church?' Culaan moved over to stand before the Priest.

'He has gone quite mad, just like his father. When he first took the throne, he returned the exiled Priests of Rome and supported a return to freedom of religion but recently, he has grown as dark and as obsessed as his father was.'

The Priest looked wistfully at the tendrils of smoke that floated from the little round window. The front door was smouldering, but the church bell was still intact. The little building was no more than twenty paces wide and probably only held twenty people. The stone was solid, but the interior, with the wooden beams and panelled walls would be ruined.

'Why do you think that is?'

The Priest thought a moment and then sighed. 'The Devil himself, I think. King Huneric hides behind a religious front. He claims he fights for Arianism, a form of our own religion but with minor, inconsequential differences. What he really wants is power and Arianism is just an excuse to kill and oppress others.'

'Others, meaning Catholics.' Culaan looked at the Priest, who nodded.

'I'm ashamed to say our religion is not much better. The Emperor in Rome grows fat with gold and gems while our people struggle to feed their families. It is a battle for power hidden behind semantics. Not the work of God.'

Culaan patted the man on the back and smiled. 'It is the way of men I'm afraid. But today, your God has given you peace. Your treasures have been saved.' The Warrior took a large sack left behind by Huneric's raid and handed it to the Priest.

He smiled a sad smile. 'These are not our treasures. These are the idols of man. The real treasure is here,' the Priest tapped Culaan's chest, 'and you have found it. The choice to save me. The love of your fellow man is the real treasure. Go in peace for the God of peace goes with you.' The Priest took the bag and walked away from the still smouldering stone building.

'I'll see to cleaning up this mess. Thank you,' he offered as he moved on.

'What about your church? Your place of worship?' Genevieve called out, as she looked back at the ruined building.

'It is just a building child. God doesn't really live there.' With that he waved his hand and continued his slow and stumbling walk to find help.

Chapter 14

The girls laughed aloud as the Prince retold a story about his hunting prowess or lack thereof. 'I'm really not cut out for that violence. My Father, like my departed Grandfather revels in it, but I'm just as happy with a group of close friends at a dinner party, or dare I say, tending the garden.' Hilderic put a finger to his lips and looked around conspiratorially as if to swear the girls to secrecy.

'Thank goodness for that.' Ariela spoke honestly. 'This place is beautiful. Is this your private garden?'

'It is part of the royal gardens. There is my room. Over there is the entrance to the King's wing and over there is where we came from, the main hall and palace entrance,' the Prince pointed with his pale, delicate hand.

The pathways were paved with granite and every corner held an ornate and luxurious water feature. The sound of trickling water was peaceful and Ariela couldn't help but feel a little homesick as the scent of flowers drifted on the warm afternoon breeze.

'So when is the King due to return?' Ariela took a sip of her watered wine and popped an olive in her mouth, another reminder of her home.

'He should return in the next day or so. He was heading to Malta for…. for business.'

'Business. What kind of business does a King do? I'm curious. I thought Kings sat on thrones while people reported to them on what was happening around their Kingdom. But what would I know?' Ariela giggled and Ophelia gave her a look that said *have you had too much to drink?*

'My Father is very active in his role. He doesn't believe the reports. He likes to see for himself.' Hilderic spoke softly. 'I try not to get involved to be honest. I'm not next in line as I said and I really hate the politics and religious friction.'

'Religious friction?' Ariela wanted to know more, from someone other than the Senator. 'My Uncle mentioned it, but told me it wasn't for *ladies* to concern themselves with such matters.' She scoffed to show her disdain.

She knew the Prince didn't want to talk about religion or politics, but she also knew that he felt somehow relegated, as women were, to the same uninformed realm of *no one cares what you think*. She didn't understand why yet, but she planned on finding out.

'It's nothing really. When Rome ruled these lands, not that they know they don't now, but the Vandals do—that's us by the way—there was only one accepted religion, Catholicism, not Judaism, not Arianism, not Hinduism, just Catholicism.'

'Why are they all isms?' Ophelia asked and everyone laughed.

'Then my Grandfather took control of this region and adopted Arianism. There really isn't a lot of difference in my opinion, but don't tell anyone I said that. I'd likely be stoned, even though I'm a prince.' A nervous giggle left the Prince's lips and Ariela smiled.

She kept her mouth shut though. She was an Israelite, what the current people of this day called a Jew, but she had yet to discover if she liked that idea or not. Religion was a contentious subject for her and that wasn't about to change.

A servant joined them and the Prince didn't speak for a moment. The young man had beautiful olive skin with dark brown thoughtful eyes and Ariela found herself smiling at his careful placement of each bowl of food and jug of wine.

'That will be all, thank you Karim.' The Prince spoke almost tenderly to the servant and Ariela couldn't help but notice the sly smile in Karim's eyes. She cocked her head at Ophelia to see if her friend had noticed but Ophelia was already putting food in her mouth.

The girl had always been curvy and loved to eat. The Priestess smiled affectionately and took a handful of nuts and seeds before relaxing back in her soft cushioned sunbed.

'Ariela, Ophelia. What on earth are you doing out here?' The Senator frowned and strode into the garden with both hands on his hips. 'You are supposed to be mingling with the dignitaries of Court. You aren't here to while away the summer in the sun.'

'Oh Uncle. The Prince was just helping me get to know the local customs. You need to relax more. Come, join us.' She patted the divan next to her. 'I'm sure you've stroked enough political egos already this afternoon.' Ariela winked at the Prince. She didn't know Victorian well yet, but she knew the man was never switched off from politics, not even for the blink of an eye.

'I think you have been hanging around Genevieve too long.' Ophelia whispered and the girls both giggled.

'The dinner is being served in the main hall. You need to come and socialise.'

'I've already loosened the laces of my dress and it isn't likely to go back in place without a servant.'

'I'll find one. I told you to keep your manners in check child, you need to come and meet a few people before we leave. You will excuse us your Highness. Ariela is a little bit of a wild child in case you hadn't noticed.' The Prince smiled his understanding.

Ariela suppressed her annoyance. The Senator was likely right. If she was to discover why she was here, she needed to get back to work, but she had been enjoying the interlude.

So far, with two trips through time, she had not had a moment to relax and enjoy life. She had promised herself that this journey would be different, especially when she found Culaan and could finally get some alone time with him.

'I'll fix your dress Ariela, and you can fix mine.'

'I ate too much. I'm not sure I can fit back into it.' Ariela placed her arms inside the long tunic and smoothed the dress on her torso as she stood.

'Ladies. This is unseemly before the Prince.' Ariela laughed aloud before placing her hand over her mouth as she had been instructed.

'I'm sorry your Highness. Please excuse our rather uncouth behaviour. We are still growing accustomed to the city life.' Ariela curtsied and the Prince smiled.

'It's been a pleasure ladies. You are always welcome to supper in my garden anytime. I'll leave you to get ready. I should be returning to the party myself, especially in my father's absence.' The Prince nodded and moved toward the main hall.

Ophelia began tightening Ariela's gown and fussing with the tunic and sash. The Priestess groaned as the laces were pulled closed and the thick sash tightened around her waist once more.

The Senator waited for the Prince to move away before he spoke. 'That was fast work ladies. How on earth did you manage a private audience with the Prince?'

'He doesn't exactly,' Ariela took a breath between Ophelia's lace tightening, 'like all the pomp and ceremony, it seems. He invited us here almost as soon as we began talking.'

The Senator frowned with suspicion. 'Maybe he knows who you are?'

'How on earth would he know that and why would he care? He is too far down the line of succession to be concerned about it in any case.' Ariela turned to tighten Ophelia's dress.

Once they were both ready, the Senator took them back to the Grand Hall. The afternoon seemed to go in slow motion from then on. The Senator introduced them to a few local merchants, one named Frumentius and a few others the Priestess struggled to find memorable. They spoke about the spice trade and local wines until Ariela thought she might pass out.

She was getting ready to insist the Senator send for a carriage when Victorian introduced her to Hilderic's cousin, Gunthamund, the next in line for the throne. He smiled graciously and kissed the back of her hand like all the men had so far. She cringed at how many germs would be infesting her hand and promised herself to wash it thoroughly as soon as she could.

'A pleasure to meet you Ariela. Victorian has told me so much about you.'

That voice. It was the man in the Senator's office. No wonder he wanted her to kill the King. She smiled the biggest smile she could to cover her reaction, but she wasn't sure he believed it.

She suddenly wished her powers included mind wiping so she could take away his suspicion but instead, she feigned a fainting spell.

She staggered a little and gripped the hand he still held. 'I am sorry. It's been a long afternoon in this heat and I'm not yet accustomed to these tight dresses. Maybe I had too much wine.'

The suspicion seemed to fall from Gunthamund's face and Ophelia moved forward to steady the Priestess, as if she might fall over at any moment.

'I'll call for a carriage Ariela. Ophelia, take my niece out for some fresh air in the courtyard and I'll get the driver to come and get you when he is ready.'

Ophelia nodded and Ariela continued to act her way free from prying eyes. 'What was that all about?' Ophelia whispered as they made their way out into the courtyard leading to the main steps.

'Gunthamund is the other voice,' Ariela whispered. 'When he took my hand and opened his mouth I stiffened. He was immediately suspicious. I had to think fast.'

'Did he believe you?'

'I'm not sure. We'll soon find out I guess.'

'Great. More enemies.'

'You wanted to come Ophelia. This is the role.'

Ophelia rolled her eyes dramatically, but she knew Ariela was right. 'It's certainly been exciting since I met you. There wasn't exactly much happening before.' She smiled and pretended to pat Ariela with concern.

A few moments later the carriage driver came for them. The Senator and Gunthamund saw the girls to the carriage and watched from the bright, shiny marble steps as they rode out of the palace gates.

'Was that an act? Did she recognise me?' Gunthamund whispered.

The Senator shook his head. 'I'm not certain. She's clever, that's for sure. Someone was in my library the other night. If it was her, I have no idea how she got there, but she has no affiliation with our enemies, not yet anyway.'

Both men turned around to return to the festivities. Neither noticed the short man with the unkempt beard delivering ale through the servant's entrance.

 **Chapter 15**

'Here, chew on this.' The Captain approached Genevieve at the bow of the ship and handed her a strange looking plant and nodded to encourage her to taste it.

She took a large bite and nearly spat it out instantly. 'Oh my lord. What is it?' She screwed up her face as she forced herself to continue chewing.

'I didn't expect you to take such a big bite.' The Captain tried to hide his mirth, but the scars on his face moved with his expression and it was impossible not to see the laughter in his eyes.

'It's like pepper, but sweet.' Genevieve continued to chew carefully.

'It's an herb. Ginger. It won't cure you, but it will help you hold down your food on the voyage home. Whenever you feel sick, chew a small amount until it's ground to nothing, then swallow it. Don't spit it out.'

Genevieve bit the piece in her mouth in half and put the rest, including the small, saliva-covered chunk in her leather pouch. The ship had sailed from port only a few moments ago and already she had felt like she was recovering from a big night on the ale, but as the ginger and saliva made its way into her stomach, she began to feel human again.

'That is amazing. Thank you. I could almost survive working on the ship now.'

'I've heard you have a new appointment.' The Captain studied her face. 'The King seems taken with your skills. News of your altercation has spread.'

Genevieve only nodded.

'He's going to want to know who paid you.'

'That's going to be difficult since no one did.'
Genevieve spoke quietly. She wasn't sure why, but she thought she could trust the Captain.

The Captain's eyes grew wide at the revelation. 'Why did you save the Priest?'

'At first, to get back in the King's employ. In the end, because the poor man didn't deserve to die for his beliefs.' The Huntress swallowed her ginger medicine and smiled. 'I feel much better now.' She moved forward, her eyes twinkling with mischief. 'Can we find somewhere a little more private to… talk?' She touched his chest and sighed.

'I have to guide the ship into open water.' The Captain didn't move away.

'But after that?' Genevieve ran her hand down the Captain's bare arm, letting her fingers linger on his skin.

'I'll see what I can manage.' He smiled at her brazen behaviour. 'You are a force to be reckoned with woman.' The Captain turned to leave.

'You better believe it Captain,' the Huntress whispered huskily.

'Omar.' He turned back to look at her. 'My name is Omar.' Genevieve nodded and smiled.

'Come and find me when you are free to *talk* Omar.'

The Huntress watched her prey move away. He swayed with the ship, his steps sure and solid on the rocking platform. He was tall and lean with skin almost as dark as night. There was something exotic about him and Genevieve felt her passion rising.

'What was that all about?' Culaan asked

'I was just making plans to keep me occupied.' Culaan shook his head at his sister.

'You're going to pick the wrong man one day sister...
that or find yourself with child.'

'I think I'm barren.' Genevieve winked. 'Can't a girl
have a little fun? You certainly had your fair share before
Ariela.'

The sound of her name made Culaan sigh. 'When I get
back, I'm going to find where she is. I miss her Genie, like I've
never missed anyone or anything.'

Genevieve reached out to the railing and patted her
brother's hand. 'We'll do what we can to make sure you two
get some time together. That Angel is a tough task master
that's for sure.'

'That he is.'

'Culaan, Genevieve.' The Captain of the guard called
up to the bow. 'The King will see you now.' Roderic's tone
was flat and his scar twitched as he spoke.

'What are we going to tell him?' Genevieve whispered.

'Leave it to me.' Culaan smiled as he slid down the
ladder to the main deck and moved up alongside the Captain
arrogantly.

'If it were up to me, I'd kill you both where you stand.'

'I'd like to see you try,' Genevieve goaded.

'Roderic isn't it?' Culaan patted the Captain on the
shoulder as he moved alongside. 'It's not up to you though, is
it?' Culaan grinned and the soldier's snarl became a pout.

The Captain knocked on the door and entered. 'The
mercenaries Sire.'

'Leave us Roderic.' The King shooed the Captain from
the room with a flurry of his hand. He hesitated a moment until
Culaan copied the King's shooing motion, a wicked smile on
his lips.

'You went to a lot of effort to regain my employment.' It wasn't a question and Genevieve wondered if the Captain had said something, but he hadn't had time to visit the King.

Culaan shrugged. 'History is written by the victors. Riches are made with the winning side. It's just common sense to want to work with the strongest.'

'Who employed you to help the Priest or was that just a ploy?'

'Just a ploy your Highness.'

'But you didn't want the Priest dead, that makes me question your loyalty.'

'Killing the weak and defenceless doesn't excite me.' Culaan looked around for a seat. There was none so he perched himself arrogantly on the edge of the monstrous wooden desk that occupied most of the room. Only a hammock swung in the corner where the Captain or the King must have usually slept.

'You have balls boy. I'll give you that. Or maybe you are just stupid.'

'Big balls,' Culaan nodded as he smiled, 'at least that's what the ladies tell me.' Genevieve rolled her eyes as he looked to her to confirm his boast.

'He has bedded every woman in our village so I'm guessing he had a big something, that's for sure.'

The King chuckled. 'You two are a perfect pigeon pair aren't you? Full of youth and arrogant bravado and naivety.'

'We aren't naïve your Highness. Arrogant, young, but not naïve. We can back up our words with our skills.'

'So you just want to work for me to become rich and powerful, but you don't like killing weak and *innocent* people? Mercenaries with morals. That is new.'

'There are plenty of rich, wicked assholes in the world to kill without picking on village Priests. Why don't you focus on the big boys?' Culaan had the beginnings of a plan forming in his mind. He held no love of Rome and the Roman Church didn't seem to be about faith, but power and money, as the Romans had always been.

'What do you propose?' The King was leaning forward, showing great interest in the Warrior's ideas. An amulet slipped from his shirt and spun in the air before the King clutched it back and tied his top shut with the leather lace as if the item didn't exist.

'I need to get a feel for the political landscape before I jump too far forward, but we,' Culaan waved toward Genevieve, 'we are worth keeping around. If we don't deliver the intelligence you require or we don't perform our duties to your satisfaction, you are welcome to terminate our employment. We don't hold grudges.'

The King smiled. 'Enjoy the trip. I'll introduce you around the Palace when I arrive. I think the King's guard isn't the right place for you two. I've got a more specialised role in mind.'

Culaan nodded understanding. The seed was planted. He'd be able to find Ariela and move freely around the city of Carthage without interference from the King's guard, especially Roderic.

'We'll be finding a meal and hammock for the night then, if it suits your Highness.' Culaan added a tip of his head before moving from the corner of the desk.

'Very well. I'll call for you if I need you.' Genevieve made for the door. 'I don't suppose you'd be interested in staying with me a little while Genevieve?'

The Huntress turned and smiled as graciously as she could possibly manage. 'I appreciate the offer your Highness, but I never mix business with pleasure.' The King nodded and the siblings left the room, Culaan gently escorting his sister with his hand on her back, a gesture not lost on the King.

The King watched the door close and unlaced his top with a sudden sense of urgency. The amulet felt warm to his touch and the sensation it gave him was intoxicating, better than bedding the Huntress could ever be. His veins pulsed with power as he stroked the hooked cross between his fingers.

Beware the warrior. The words echoed in his mind and he smiled, feeling the tingling sensation surge through his body.

# Chapter 16

Matias waited for the King's ship to dock. The wharf erupted into activity as the vessel arrived and ropes were thrown from the deck as men rushed around to secure the vast vessel.

He watched the foreigners make their way down the gangplank, wondering again if he was making the right decision.

Culaan looked to the food stall, hoping to catch a glimpse of Tias. 'Good Sir. Can I interest you in a roast meat roll?' Matias called as Culaan made eye contact.

'Sounds delicious.' Culaan and Genevieve pushed through the throng of activity to the stall and took the food from Matias.

'Good to see you both still breathing.' The stall holder grinned.

'It was close for a moment but we are still here.' Genevieve shrugged casually in admission.

'You know what we spoke about last time?' The Warrior nodded. 'Well, things might have changed a little. I've also seen your friend.' Culaan raised a questioning eyebrow.

'We are just on our way for an ale. This roll is just what we needed.' Matias nodded his understanding and the pair left to make their way further down the dock toward the tavern.

'I thought we were doing the spying?' Genevieve asked.

'Seems Tias likes all the cloak and dagger mystery. Let's find out what he knows, especially about Ariela.'

Culaan ordered two ales and a platter of cheese and dried fruit. The rolls were delicious, but greasy and he needed to break up the lump of meat in his gut.

The waitress, who had been less than hospitable last time, was now all smiles. She batted her eyelashes and flipped her hair around with every word. Genevieve openly rolled her eyes, sending the waitress on her way quickly.

'Now she knows you've got money, she's all over you. I know her type. Tramp.'

'I'm not interested anyway Genie. I'm sure she isn't a tramp though, probably just trying to feed a hungry family.'

They had finished their ale and the barmaid was on her way over with another when Matias joined them. They chose the same table, with the clear view of the entrance and both sat on the far side, facing Matias.

'Your friend is a ward of the Senator of Hadrumetum. He has an estate near the Palace.'

'You saw her? Did she look well? Unharmed?' Culaan chewed his fingernail nervously.

'She is your woman.' Matias smiled knowingly. Culaan scowled, so he quickly answered the question. 'She looked fine, happy, chatting with a big busted girl with impossibly red lips and dark skin.'

'Ophelia. They are together.' Genevieve took a sip of her ale.

'Another friend of yours. Very good. You spy on you know who, and they can spy on the Senator.' Matias looked behind him to make sure no one could overhear.

'What's your game in all of this Matias? The Catholics and the Arians or should we say the Vandals and the Romans, that's what this is really about, who rules in Carthage?' Culaan held the man in his intense gaze. 'What's in it for you?'

'I told you before I'm not interested in the politics but while the King was away, I saw the Senator being very chummy with Gunthamund, the King's Cousin. I think there is an alliance between them.'

'Again, what's it to you?'

Matias scrunched his nose as he debated exactly how much he should trust these two foreign warriors. He had seen the flicker of light when Culaan had drawn his sword on that first day. It had sent shivers down his spine and he knew there was more to both of them than they were sharing.

'I think it best to show you my secret, then maybe you will be secure enough to trust me and show me yours.'

Culaan frowned at Genevieve but chose not to answer the questions.

'Drink your ale and then leave the tavern. Turn right down the first lane. Follow the alley until you come to a dead end. Wait there and I'll join you as soon as I make sure no one has followed you.'

Matias didn't wait for an answer. Instead, he stood to leave the tavern, casually chatting with a few patrons who sat along his path. They all knew him well. He patted a big bronzed sailor on the back, and slapped a woman on the backside. She giggled at his words as he tipped his head to her.

Culaan watched the short, stout man move. He wasn't a warrior, of that there was no doubt, but there was something in the way he held himself that nudged Culaan to be wary.

'What do you make of that?' Genevieve hadn't taken her eyes off the stall holder until he walked out of sight.

'I think there is a lot more to Matias than we thought.' He took a long, slow swig of his ale, trying to wait, but his nerves were tingling.

'Are you going to finish that?' Genevieve put her hand on his half-finished mug. He shook his head and she guzzled the remaining amber liquid in one, long, slow mouthful.

'Time to go,' she smiled as she nudged her brother from his seat. 'Let's discover his *secret* then.'

****

'What are you doing Hilderic? I've told you before, you don't do gardening with beautiful women, you bed them boy.' The King strode into the Palace garden, his sword still strapped to his side, his black leather armour on full display.

The Prince stood up from the vegetable garden, ignoring his father's crass comment as though it was common practice.

Ariela did everything she could to quell the outrage that must have shown on her face before rising to her feet and brushing off the dirt from her dress. How they had managed to convince Idris that more practical and comfortable clothing was in order for today's visit was a miracle in itself.

Ophelia chuckled as if she knew some great secret, but dusted off her hands and turned to face their visitor.

The Priestess fixed an accusatory gaze on her friend, who only shrugged that she wasn't yet ready to share her revelation.

'Ariela, Ophelia, let me introduce you to the King of the Vandals and ruler of Carthage.' Huneric puffed out his already enormous chest and lifted his chin a notch higher.

Ariela and Ophelia curtsied. 'We would have cleaned ourselves up had we known you would be joining us your Highness.' Ariela hoped her tone was sweet, but Ophelia's grin told her it wasn't.

'Ladies. A pleasure to meet you both. Where ever did you find these beauties Hilderic?'

Once again, the Prince ignored his father's tone. 'Ariela is Senator Victorian's niece and Ophelia is her closest friend.'

The King's features grew dark at the mention of Victorian's name. Ariela felt the hairs on the back of her neck stand on end but it was Ophelia's expression that caught her off guard.

Her friend's eyes had gone from a squint to wide open and she had grown slightly pale. Ariela put her arm around her shoulders. 'Are you alright?'

Ophelia snapped to attention as though falling from a trance. 'Yes, yes, I'm sorry. Just a little dizzy. I must have stood up too quickly.'

The King suppressed his sudden rage and took a deep breath. 'You must bring these lovely ladies to dinner this evening Hilderic.' The Prince made to object but the King put up his hand. 'I must insist.' The condescending tone was back.

'Very well father. I will have to ensure the Senator gives his permission of course.'

'You will do nothing of the sort. Senator Victorian is here by *my* good grace and he understands the rules.' The King turned on his heel and strode from the garden. The Prince sighed loudly.

'I'm sorry Ariela, Ophelia.' Hilderic tipped his head. 'If you haven't already noticed, my father isn't exactly accustomed to not getting what he wants. Would you do me the honour of joining me for dinner in the King's private dining room?'

Ariela didn't know why, but the pit of her stomach was rolling at the thought. The hairs still stood to attention at the back of her neck and Ophelia still held her arm firmly, as she had when they had dived into the portal to come to this time.

She forced a pleasant smile to her lips. 'It would be a pleasure.' The Prince let out a breath, as if he thought that they might actually refuse. 'I'm sure my Uncle will be fine. He is the one who insisted I make myself known in the King's court.' Ariela giggled, which sounded hollow even to her own ears, but the Prince didn't seem to notice.

# Chapter 17

Culaan waited impatiently. The dark blue door at the end of the alleyway stood closed. There were stone stairs leading up either side of the alley to more doors, but no one was about, not even a stray cat or dog.

Genevieve and Culaan jumped at the sound, but neither could make out where it was coming from. A chuckle made Genevieve look up to find Matias scampering along the roof line with an agility that belied his build. When he reached the stairway on the left of the alley, he vaulted to the landing with little effort.

'You are full of surprises little man.' Culaan grinned as the stall holder jumped the railing and landed in the alley before them.

'That's nothing. Wait until you see what comes next.' Matias returned the grin with the mischief of a youth.

Culaan expected him to knock on the big blue door, but instead, he went around the back of the stairs he had vaulted over and waved them to follow. When they were all out of sight, he tapped the wall, which disappeared.

Genevieve sucked in a quick breath 'Magic.'

Matias chuckled. 'Something I think you two are very familiar with.' He ducked through the doorway and the warriors followed. The light of day disappeared as soon as they passed the threshold, but all along the wall stood balls of light, not unlike the ones Ariela could manifest.

'Follow me.' Matias started moving down the long stone corridor. The ground was sloping down, Culaan was sure of it. The descent was gradual and the temperature dropped slowly, but they were at least a full building height below ground when the corridor opened into a large cavern.

'Welcome to Shiloh.' Matias grinned.

'Shiloh?' Culaan cocked his head as two women, around Ariela's age moved forward offering them a drink of water. They both wore short tunics under long woollen, hooded cloaks.

'Yes. You have heard of it?' Matias was seeking the extent of their knowledge. Culaan hesitated for only a second. If the stall holder hadn't given them up the moment he realised they were familiar with magic, then he wasn't about to hand them over to the King or the Senator now.

'Yes. We have.' Ariela had told them both about where she had come from and the Order her mother had created.

'Our friend is from your Order.' Culaan offered, unsure if he should divulge too much.

Matias grinned. 'I had hoped as much. Her coming was foretold, but it seems the Senator has gotten to her first.'

'Gotten to her. That doesn't sound good.'

'She is safe. They want her power. They want her to kill the King for them. They will not harm her, even if they could, and I don't think they could. Her history to this point had been written in our scrolls and we will continue to write it for future generations.'

'So you know who we are then.' Genevieve focussed on Matias as Culaan took a sip from his cup of water.

'Come, we will sit for a while. I'll tell you what I know and you can share what you want if you choose to.'

Matias walked toward a stone archway at the end of the cavern. He passed a group of small children, playing knuckle-bones on the dirt floor.

'How do you keep this place hidden with children hanging about? They are not known for their ability to keep secrets.' Culaan handed his cup to one of the girls who followed them, their faces partly hidden by their hoods.

'The children only know we feed them. They are hungry orphans, made so by the war between the Vandals and the Romans. They are street urchins, forced to steel to feed themselves and their families. They will not betray us because we make sure they don't go hungry and we tend to their health.'

'I hope you are right,' Genevieve whispered.

'The Senator knows we exist. He thinks his faction is more powerful than ours, so he remains arrogant and ignores our comings and goings.'

They moved through the archway and into another corridor. More magical balls of light shone on the walls, framing doorways of dark wood. When they reached the end, Matias opened a double set of doors and ushered them through.

'You have a palace down here,' Culaan remarked as he moved into the room. Even without natural light, the room shone with daylight. There was a divan in the corner, a small table, walls hung with rugs and a large oak desk was on the far side.

Matias ignored the comment, instead, he directed the siblings to the divan. 'Bring us some refreshments girls. There is no need to stand guard today.' The hooded figures bowed and left as Culaan suddenly realised they were not there to greet him, but to protect Matias if the need arose.

'If they possess even a small amount of Ariela's power then I am glad they didn't see us as a threat,' Culaan smiled. 'So, you know who we are.' He pushed on, remembering Genevieve's earlier question.

'I believe I do. Your names were recorded in history and I saw the flash when you drew your sword on our first meeting. I just needed to be sure before I brought you here.'

'What makes you sure now?' Genevieve leant back into the divan, beginning to relax.

'The King didn't kill you and I'm running out of time. Like I said, the Senator and Gunthamund are up to something and as bad as Huneric is, I'm not sure having Victorian pulling Gunthamund's strings would be any better.'

'What do you want from us?' Culaan looked to the doors as the two guards returned with food.

'Thank you, girls. That will be all.' Matias spoke respectfully to the Priestesses, who nodded and left without a word.

'Do you lead the Priestesses?' Genevieve popped a piece of fruit in her mouth.

'I don't. I protect the Order. I'm just a thief really, like those children out there.' Matias waved his hand at the now closed doors. 'They took me in and sheltered me.'

'So who leads now?' Culaan sat forward in his seat to reach for a handful of nuts.

'The Order splintered into two factions when I was young. Senator Victorian misguiding one faction and a Priestess named Deborah guiding this one.'

'What makes you so sure Deborah guides the correct faction?' Genevieve's interest was piquing.

'Deborah passed many years ago. I knew her well. I trusted her, but more than that, I was with her when the Angel Raziel came to her. I don't believe the Angel would have shared Ariela's prophecy with Victorian.'

'How then did Victorian find out about it?' All the intrigue was beginning to excite Culaan.

'When the Senator left, he took some of our most skilled fighting Priestesses with him, but we are not sure if it was accidental or on purpose, a few less than honourable Priestesses remained.'

'He left spies.' Genevieve looked at Culaan. 'A smart man.'

'Smart and ruthless. Shortly after we discovered the prophecy had been shared with Victorian, Deborah died in a freak *accident*.'

'You believe the Senator had her killed?' Culaan looked at Matias with sympathy.

'I gave away any idea of proving or disproving anything years ago. I'm the only living person who knows the extent of what the Angel shared that night.'

Culaan let the information filter in for a moment. 'So, what did the Angel say?'

'He said that the King wasn't evil, but the amulet was. He said Ariela would need to secure the artefact, for to kill the King would be against the Order's mandate.'

'Ariela would never kill anyone for political control, but if she though he were evil, she might. What amulet was Raziel talking about? Did he describe it?' Culaan looked at Genevieve, who nodded she was thinking the same thing.

'I have no idea,' Matias chuckled.

'Well, we might be able to help.' Matias looked from Culaan to Genevieve and took a slow breath as a look of hope filled his eyes.

Chapter 18

Culaan and Genevieve waited at the guard's entrance to the Palace. They had been given no papers, or anything to show the commander, but the Captain and the King had both assured them, they wouldn't have any issues getting into the Palace.

The Guard on duty sent a runner to the Captain of the King's guard who arrived a few moments later.

'The King is expecting you.' Roderic did nothing to hide his disdain but Culaan could hardly blame him, they had killed five of his men in Malta and were now being given a favourable position that the Captain would have no control over.

Without another word, Roderic waved them through and nodded to the guard to allow them to pass.

'This is going to be fun,' Genevieve whispered so only Culaan could hear, but there was no amusement in her voice.

It was late in the afternoon on a warm day and Culaan wondered just how hot the black leather armour of the King's guard was. He smiled thinking about how happy he was that he wasn't going to have to wear it.

'What are you so happy about?' Genevieve spoke in her normal voice, not bothering if the Captain heard.

'At least we don't have to wear that hot, back armour.' Culaan nodded toward the man leading them. Genevieve giggled.

'The King has dinner guests in a few hours, so he will see you now.' The Captain opened a pair of doors that led into the side of an expansive garden. They followed him down a marble pathway leading into the main palace.

'Are you lost yet?' Genevieve's question was genuine. She was an excellent hunter in the wild, but when it came to the inside of these huge buildings, she was quickly disorientated.

'The hallways all run in a grid pattern at least. I've got a fairly good idea of where we are in relation to where we came in.'

They walked past a large dining room, laid out for the meal that the Captain had mentioned. At the end of the long hallway, Roderic opened the doors to a lavishly decorated meeting room.

On the other side of the main room, another set of double doors was already open. Inside, the King sat at a desk almost as big as his dining table.

'Genevieve, Culaan, take a seat. That will be all thank you Roderic.' The man bowed, but while the King was still busy moving scrolls and maps around his table, the Captain didn't miss the opportunity to snarl at the two newcomers.

A few more moments passed after the Captain left, before the King put away what he had been working on and gave them his full attention. 'You are probably wondering what I've got in order for you first up?'

Both warriors nodded. 'We are at your disposal your Highness.' Culaan offered with as much genuine emotion as he could muster and a slight bow of his head.

'Tonight, I want you to dine with me. Strange I know, but the niece of a man I believe to be my enemy is getting very close to my son and I need to make sure she isn't a part of Victorian's plans.'

Culaan didn't know how to react… Ariela, getting close to another man. That wasn't what he had hoped to hear.

Genevieve picked up on his thoughts and spoke for them both. 'What time do you want us to arrive?'

'Shortly after the sun sets and Genevieve, you'll need to find a dress. I'll send someone to attend to you when we finish up here.' He grinned knowing the Huntress was not about to enjoy being dressed up like the ladies of his court.

'You need to blend in as well as the other guests, not one of my spies, not one of my soldiers. Culaan, I'll have suitable clothing organised for you as well.'

Culaan forced himself to focus and bowed his head in acknowledgement to the King's wishes. 'Should we know more about your suspicions regarding this enemy you speak of?' The Warrior had a fairly good idea, but he wanted to see just how much the King was willing to share.

'The Senator of Hadrumetum, Victorian and my nephew, Gunthamund have been seen meeting too much behind closed doors. I'm not sure, but I have a sneaking suspicion, as Gunthamund is next in line, that he might be planning something sinister.'

'Is there a reason for them to want you out of the way?'

'Victorian is a Roman merchant. His family is said to be loyal to Rome, but at the very least, he is loyal to the Catholics and let's say I'm not exactly popular with them at the moment.' The King smiled at his obvious statement.

'Why are you persecuting the Catholics, if you don't mind me asking your Highness?' Culaan was testing the limits of his new relationship with the King, but he needed to know the man's motives.

'It's political. I honestly don't care about the semantics of the religions, but it makes for a great pivotal point for the fanatics to stew over. It gives me an excuse to take the wealth from the Romans without bringing war with Rome down on

Carthage. There's nothing better than a religious or racial squabble to distract everyone from the real political game.'

Culaan had suspected as much. The King didn't seem the religious zealot type. He nodded and smiled to make the King feel at ease with the information shared.

'Are there any other guests except the Senator's niece?'

'Just her friend, my son and Gunthamund and his wife.'

Culaan raised an eyebrow at the guest list. If Gunthamund was going to be there, he had better be prepared. 'Does your son know who we are?'

The King shook his head. 'No. Hilderic is a little soft when it comes to politics. I'm not expecting him to have to rule. Gunthamund will take the crown when I retire, but I don't want a Roman sympathiser controlling him when he does.'

****

'What is bothering you?' Ophelia had refused to say anything until they were back in Ariela's room in the Senator's estate.

'Not in here.' Ophelia opened the double doors leading to the balcony and took a seat at Ariela's white-painted iron table and chairs.

Ariela huffed as she joined her. 'You look as pale as this furniture. What is going on?'

'The King. He has an amulet, of great power. I couldn't feel it until Hilderic mentioned the Senator and then it hit me like a ball of fire. Whatever it is, it feeds on his rage or maybe his insecurities.'

'I felt something, but nothing that violent.'

'I am the Guardian of Relics after all. I might not throw fireballs, but I know a relic of power when I feel one. He must keep it hidden on his person somewhere.'

'That is going to make it very difficult to get it away from him. That must be what we are here for, the Relic. Nothing to do with the Catholic and Arian feud. It's all just a smoke screen.'

'Do you think Victorian knows about the Relic?' Ophelia offered.

'Let's hope not. So far all I heard him and Gunthamund talking about was killing the King. We can leave them to be side tracked by that, while we secure the relic.' Ariela got to her feet.

'I need to find Idris and see what she knows. This is getting messy. Victorian has taken my Mother's Order and distorted it. This was never what she would have wanted.'

'You don't need to go anywhere. I'm sure Victorian has heard about our dinner party by now. Idris won't be too far away. She'll either be spying on us or at the very least, getting us all prised up for the dinner.' Ophelia chuckled quietly.

'True.' As if on cue, Idris knocked on the door.

'Come in Idris.' Both girls said at the same time. The Priestess come servant opened the door with a surprised look on her face.

'How did you know it was me? Was it your gift?'

Both girls laughed out loud as Idris stood by, her mouth and eyes wide with confusion.

Chapter 19

Ariela and Ophelia were shown to the King's dining room by a well-rounded woman in her middle years.

'The King has only a few guests with him this evening. It will be a lovely, intimate affair where you should be able to get to know the King and the Prince of course.'

Ariela resisted the urge to roll her eyes. She knew the Prince was not the least bit interested in her, especially romantically and even if he were, she'd not be pursuing him, even if the Senator wanted her to.

Seats scraped back as the girls entered the dining room, all but the King's. He remained seated, regarding her with a look that unnerved the Priestess a little.

Ariela heard someone clear their throat. Her eyes fell on Culaan who had deliberately tried to get her attention. It took all her will power not to run into his arms, but on the inside her heart leapt into her throat. Why hadn't she felt his presence?

'Hilderic. You can make the introductions.' The King nodded for everyone to be seated, as servants pulled out a chair for each of the two girls.

Ariela struggled to tuck her excessively full skirt under the table. Culaan grinned, and without any special gifts, she knew exactly what he was thinking. He tried to keep the mix of passion and amusement from his eyes, but she could read it.

His golden hair was tied back, low on his neck with a piece of leather. He wore a white long-sleeved shirt under a midnight blue tunic. The cuff of the long sleeves was embroidered with golden symbols and the ruffled ends of his shirt peaked out from underneath. The colour was perfect, highlighting his beautiful blue eyes.

She shut her eyes to block out her view and turned to Hilderic, next to whom she had been seated. He had begun the introductions and she hoped she hadn't missed anything. When she glanced at the King, his eyes were fixed on her, the feeling of discomfort hadn't abated.

'You've met the King of course. This is my cousin Gunthamund.' The man nodded his head. 'His wife, Gwen.' The woman looked as though she'd swallowed turned milk. Her eyes, like the King's burrowed into her.

Ariela wondered where the Queen was, but didn't ask. Something to talk privately with Hilderic about later.

'These are two of my father's,' the Prince seemed to be trying to find the right word, 'personal advisors, Genevieve and Culaan.'

Culaan sat directly opposite Ariela, Genevieve at his side.

'Everyone, this is the Senator's niece Ariela and her closest friend Ophelia.'

A few pleasantries were shared as a servant poured wine into everyone's glass. Ariela admired the workmanship. She'd never seen anything like it. They were so fine, the vision through the glass was almost unobscured. The base was wide enough to balance the tall stem and large volume of liquid that sat above. She was nervous, that at any moment, it might fall over and spill the contents on the King's pristine white linen tablecloth.

Hilderic smiled at the careful way she lifted the glass to her lips. As she took a sip, he nodded encouragingly, somehow knowing she wasn't accustomed to the glass. Ophelia copied her actions, then Genevieve and Culaan.

The Warrior watched her over his glass, his eyes
moving from Hilderic and back to her. She raised an eyebrow
slightly at him, understanding why his smile had suddenly
turned to a frown.

'So, Culaan, exactly about what are you offering advice
to our King?' Gunthamund sat at the opposite end of the table
to the King, who now glared at the man.

Culaan looked to the King for guidance. 'Our work is
of a confidential nature. I'm sure the King will share it with
those who need to know.'

'You look like a warrior boy. You're built like an ox
and your friend here, Genevieve was it,' no-one responded, so
Gunthamund continued, undeterred, 'she's no lady of the court
I'm sure.'

'Gunthamund. I didn't invite you here to insult my
guests.' The King began eating the first course. Ariela studied
the tiny little chicken wings and watched as Hilderic gently
coaxed the meat of the bones with a sharp knife that he
collected from the right of his fine, handcrafted porcelain plate.
The other side of the wing, he held delicately with his left
hand.

Culaan's smile had returned as he watched the two men
argue. It was obvious they were not close friends and that the
King had no intention of hiding the nature of his and
Genevieve's employment, fancy outfits or not. He collected up
his tiny wings and sucked the meat off them in one mouthful.

Genevieve glared at him. Ariela could see she wished to
do the same, but instead, she took the knife and delicately pried
the meat off the bone.

'No, you invited me here to introduce your spies.'

'What Culaan and Genevieve are tasked with is nothing
to do with you. But if they were spies, you'd have nothing to

be so bothered about, unless of course you are hiding something.'

Gunthamund must have realised he'd pushed the matter too far. He lifted his hand in the air in mock surrender. 'You are quite right. It's none of my business who you employ to offer their expertise and advice.'

There was an unsteady silence and Ariela nearly giggled. The servant had said it was to be an intimate dinner, but it was beginning to look like a rather uncomfortable kind of intimacy.

'How was your day Ariela?' Hilderic asked politely and all eyes fell upon her.

'Well, after we left our little gardening session with you, Ophelia and I spent most of the afternoon getting ready for this evening.'

Everyone laughed and the tension was eased, except when Ariela looked at Culaan, she could see his intense gaze. Genevieve must have noticed his sullen expression which she appeared to have answered with a kick under the table.

'So, you are brother and sister.' Hilderic continued to draw the conversation along and away from politics. Ariela smiled at him, silently thanking him for his consideration. It seemed diplomacy was not so foreign to him afterall.

'Yes.' Culaan's words drew her attention once more and she gently shook her head to try and dispel his growing jealously.

'We grew up as friends, but discovered only recently that we are twin siblings.' Genevieve took another sip of her wine and encouraged Culaan to do the same with a nod. 'This is very good wine. Is it locally grown?'

The conversation continued into the evening pleasantly until the King called an end to dinner. 'Hilderic. Why don't you take Ariela out into the garden while I speak with my new advisers?'

Culaan stiffened as Hilderic pulled Ariela's chair away for her to stand. Her legs were almost numb, having been shoved between the seat and the table with volumes of fabric. As she made to move, her legs gave out and Hilderic wrapped his arm around her waist to stop her from falling.

Ophelia came to her aid and Ariela saw Culaan move, but Genevieve put a hand on his arm to stop him.

'Where are we to stay this evening?' Genevieve asked loud enough for Ariela to hear. At least she was keeping her head in the game. Culaan seemed to have totally lost focus.

'We'll discuss that shortly my dear. I have some work for you to do first. Your evening has only just begun.'

 **Chapter 20**

'You see my nephew is a little wary of you already.' The King smiled as he walked with Culaan and Genevieve toward the west wing of the palace.

'I'm not sure why you had us dress up so fine your Highness, you knew we would stand out in any case. I think your intimidation techniques might have done the trick though.' Genevieve smiled, hoping to make the King feel confident in their loyalty.

'I won't admit to anything.' Hilderic returned the Huntress's smile. 'You'll both stay here. You can come and go through the west gate. The guards will have orders to let you pass.'

'What do you need us to do tonight?'

'Follow Ariela when she leaves. Find out how entrenched in Victorian's plans she is.'

'She doesn't look like politics is really her forté your Highness.' Genevieve tried to dispel his concerns. The last thing they needed was for the Priestess to be under suspicion.

'However, we'll double check of course.' Culaan offered his support and Genevieve questioned him with her eyes.

'Here is your apartment. Report back to me first thing in the morning. You'll find me in my study at daybreak.'

The King left them standing in the corridor. 'What was that all about?'

'I needed a reason to go and see Ariela. What better one than on the order of the King?'

Genevieve took a deep breath. 'Yes, but you didn't need to throw the girl into suspicion to do so. He'd have sent us to follow her in any case.'

Culaan opened the door to the room, expecting a single cell with a bed each. Instead, he found a vast living room, lit by wall lamps and filled with soft divans, a fireplace and glass doors leading to a long balcony.

Two rooms led from each end of the living room, one had Genevieve's belongings already stacked neatly on the bed, the other held Culaan's.

'I could get used to this.' Genevieve offered as she leapt onto the bed and smiled at her brother. She then bounced back up and closed the doors to get changed.

Moments later she returned dressed in her leather trousers, a green woodsman's tunic over the top and her bow slung over her shoulder.

Culaan changed from his formal wear into his own street clothing and returned to the living room. He took the lid from a heavy glass decanter and smelled the contents.

'Rum. Do you want one before we go? I think it might be a little while before mister fancy pants lets my girl go home.' Culaan sulked waiting for Genie to answer.

'Yes, I'll have one.' His sister moved toward the side table and took the glass from his hand. 'You know she is only playing along, getting to know the Prince so she can work out what our mission is here?'

'Maybe. But she doesn't have to look like she's enjoying it so much.'

****

Ariela climbed into the carriage first, dragging her voluminous train of fabric with her as Ophelia followed in the same manner.

107

'He's sweet.' Ariela spoke as the carriage jolted and the horses drew them out of the Palace and back to the Senator's estate.

'Don't let Culaan hear you say that. Did you see his face?' Ophelia giggled.

'Yes. I hope only we saw his reaction. He was being a twit. He knows I'm only interested in him.'

'Does he?'

'Oh I hope so. I've seen him get rowdy and it isn't pretty.'

'How are we going to get that amulet from you know who?' Ophelia drew the curtain back on the carriage and peered out to make sure the footman wasn't riding on the side-step as he sometimes did.

'Was he wearing it tonight?'

'Yes. I didn't see it, but I could feel it.'

'That makes sense. I was trying all night to speak to Culaan through the ethereal, but I couldn't reach him. I wasn't sure if it was because he was being pig headed or because of the amulet.'

'The amulet I'd say. I don't know what it is, what it looks like or even why it's so powerful. You are going to have to ask Culaan and Genevieve to see if they have seen it.'

'How on earth are we going to manage communicating with them if I can't reach Culaan with my gift?'

'He'll have to leave the palace at some point. You can try and sense him then.'

The carriage pulled up inside the Estate grounds and Idris met them.

'Don't you ever sleep?' Ariela asked as the Senator's most trusted servant held out his hand to help the Priestess down from the carriage.

The woman chuckled. 'Of course, I sleep. Just not too long,' she smiled. The Senator wanted a report on how you are progressing with Hilderic.'

'The Senator can wait until the morning. I'm exhausted.'

'I'll need to tell him something.'

Ariela sighed. 'Tell him the Prince is very hospitable. I'm not sure he knows much about the political state of Carthage or the King's plans against the Catholics though. I'll know more in time.'

'Thank you. I'll let you ladies both get to bed. You know the way.' They nodded and lifted their long skirts to navigate the marble stairs up into the courtyard entrance. As Ariela walked through the hanging garden, she began to relax and let her spirit wander in search of Culaan.

****

Culaan and Genevieve watched the girls disappear inside the grand entry hall. They had no idea where Ariela's room would be.

'We should circle the building. You go that way; I'll meet you on the other side. They'll have to light the lanterns when they enter their rooms.'

Genevieve nodded. 'It's a long way up those walls Culaan. How are you going to reach them?'

'We, how are *we* going to reach them?' Culaan grinned.

Genevieve chuckled 'I don't think so.'

On the ocean side of the massive structure, Culaan saw two rooms light up at the same time. He could just make out a figure on one of the balconies. He took a deep, long breath and focussed on Ariela, her scent, her long dark hair, her beautiful almost black eyes.

Culaan. Where are you?

Look down.

Genevieve joined Culaan as Ariela looked down. She was at least four or five storeys up, but he could see, or could he feel her smiling?

'She's happy to see me.' He stated with a goofy look on his face.

'Of course she is you idiot. I told you she would be.'

Can you get up here?

'No. I can't see how.' Culaan spoke aloud so Genie could hear him. He was still mastering his inside voice anyway.

'Is she communicating with you?' Culaan nodded at Genevieve's question.

I'll have to come down to you.

'That's pretty risky. Someone might see you, or us.' Culaan looked at Genevieve. 'Can you see a way up to her?'

Genevieve moved into the shadow of the wall and tried to put her fingers into the nooks of the stones to see if she could get a handhold from which to climb. She reached for a few, trying to place her soft leather boots into the nooks, but finally shook her head.

'You forget. I can travel where-ever I want.' Culaan jumped at the sound of Ariela's voice just behind his shoulder. He spun and lifted the Priestess from her feet kissing her firmly on the lips.

'You are amazing.' His voice was husky as he ran his hand down Ariela's back to pull her once more into a tight embrace.

'You're not so bad yourself.' She smiled as he touched his forehead to hers.

Genevieve cleared her throat and stepped out of the darkness, making Ariela giggle softly. 'I can't stay long, neither can you. There will be guards doing their rounds soon.'

'What's with you and the Prince?' Culaan pulled back from Ariela to study her face in the moonlight.

'Really? You want to go there now? What about why are you working for the King?'

'We were separated and landed in the King's service far too easily for it not to be divine intervention.'

'Ophelia says he has an artefact of great power. Have you seen anything?'

'Yes, I think so, an amulet. It is a hooked cross that he wears around his neck, always, but he keeps it hidden under his shirt.'

Genevieve pried the Priestess from Culaan's grip and hugged her. 'It was very enjoyable watching you flirt with the Prince. I thought Culaan was going to leap across the table at one point.'

'I wasn't flirting.' Ariela put her hands on her hips.

'Yes you were.' Culaan tried to reach for her once more, but she slapped his hand away.

'The Senator wants me to get close, so I'm just playing my part. I won't let it go anywhere.'

Culaan stepped forward, studying her face. He wrapped his hands around her cheeks and brushed her lips with his. She moaned softly as his lips skipped across her cheek and back to her lips once more.

'You know how much I love you.' Culaan looked into her eyes, his forehead almost touching hers.

She nodded slowly, then reached up and pulled him to her lips. 'I'm yours Culaan, you know that.' She breathed as the chance came to her.

'Ok you two. Back to business. If you haven't seen the artefact, how do you know it exists?'

Ariela didn't speak for a moment, but finally dragged her gaze from Culaan's eyes, to look at Genevieve. 'Ophelia.

She has felt it and I can't use my gifts around it. That's why I couldn't talk to Culaan or even sense his presence. Now we know what it looks like, she might know more about it.'

'We have been employed by the King to act as his spies, assassins if need be. Not sure yet who he wants to kill though.' Genevieve shrugged her shoulders. 'So far, we've seen him attacking the Catholic Priests, mostly on the island of Malta, but word has it he has been after them on the mainland too.'

'What on earth for?'

'Gold, why else?'

'The Senator is a religious zealot. I overheard a meeting between him and Gunthamund. They are expecting me to kill the King,' she whispered, suddenly wary of anyone overhearing.

'The King employed us because he knows the Senator and Gunthamund are up to something. He sent us to watch you. Very convenient for me, but you need to be careful.' Culaan pulled her close once more, kissing the top of her head and savouring the smell of her lavender scented hair.

'They are both insane. I don't think we are here to fight a war Culaan.'

'What's the plan then?'

'The artefact. We need to find out more.'

'We have met someone who might be able to help. It seems your mother's Order has broken into two factions. The Senator leads one, while the other is aimlessly trying to regroup, but our friend says the *amulet* is evil, not the King.'

'Evil is what we are here for Culaan. See if you can find out more.'

'We will, but you need to ask your new boyfriend if he knows anything.' Genevieve teased and nudged Culaan's arm.

He didn't look amused but that didn't deter Genevieve's wide grin.

'Can you give us a moment Genie? We can check the perimeter before we leave. Make sure we have something to report to the King.'

Genevieve nodded and moved away, making her way around the building once more.

'I can't contact you when the amulet is near. You'll need to get away from the King so we can communicate regularly.'

Culaan took Ariela's face in his hands once more and kissed her lips softly. 'I'll make sure I can sense you every evening even if I have to hike to the top of the mountain to be far enough from the King.'

'Oh Culaan. Are we ever going to get a moment to ourselves?'

'I've already told Raziel it's part of the deal this time around. I'll find time. I promise.' Ariela wrapped her arms around his neck and touched his pony tail.

'I like the look by the way. You were so handsome in that dinner jacket.' She pulled him to her, kissing his lips firmly.

'You had best stop that or I'll have to remove you from that pretty dress you're wearing.'

'Promises, promises.'

Culaan pushed her against the wall, untying her hair and running his fingers through it. 'You have no idea what you do to me Ariela. It's like torture being away from you.'

'I know the feeling. Trust me, I know.' She pulled him close as his hands began to wander over her body. 'You had better go before the guards come.'

'I'll be back tomorrow night. Where can I meet you?'

‘I’ll think of somewhere. Contact me as soon as you can.’ Culaan nearly crashed into the wall as she disappeared. The sound of voices drifted on the still night air as Culaan moved into the hedge surrounding the wall.

# Chapter 21

Idris brushed Ariela's hair and began braiding it. The Priestess squirmed in her seat, unused to the personal attention. She thought about what Culaan had told her the night before. Two factions of the Order and one led by a man, not a Priestess. Her stomach churned at the idea.

'How long have you been part of the Order Idris?'

The woman looked up from her work and studied the Priestess in the bronze mirror on the dressing table.

'As long as I can remember. When I was orphaned, the Order took me in, trained me to fight.'

'Have you always worked with the Senator?'

'No. He enlisted my help after the Catholic Priests began to go missing.'

'Missing?'

Idris nodded and tapped the Priestess on the shoulder. 'You are all ready now.'

'You said Priests went missing?'

Idris didn't seem to want to elaborate. Her brow furrowed, as though she had already said too much.

'The King has been cleansing Carthage of the Catholics for many years now and his father before him. The Senator has been doing what he can to warn them, but recently he became concerned for his life, so he called for my aid.'

'And the Order approved?'

'Yes. Of course they did. The Senator leads the Order, has done for many years now.'

'I don't understand.' Ariela stared at Idris in the mirror. 'My mother abhorred politics and loathed fighting over matters of faith even more. She would never approve of Priestesses working with politicians and merchants.'

'Then what was the Order created for if not to fight for what is right?'

'Idris, who gets to choose what is right? The Order was created to fight evil, true evil, demons, those who would use what you would call dark magic.'

'Demons. They are fairy tales told to scare children. The real monsters are people like Huneric, who use their power to kill men of faith.'

'Idris, my mother did not create the Order to choose sides in political or religious struggles. I only left her a few months ago. I know exactly what the Order was doing and it wasn't deciding who ruled. It was also never meant to be led by a politician; it was only ever to be led by a High Priestess.'

Idris bit her lip, looking uncomfortably at Ariela's reflection in the mirror. She shook her head, as though trying to clear her thoughts. 'It is time for you to attend the palace once more. The Senator needs to know if the Prince can be manipulated.'

Ariela stood as Idris began to pull the stool away, forcing her to her feet.

'I'd like to visit the Order's training grounds when I return. Please find the Senator and convey my request.'

'We no longer have a training ground.' Idris opened the door for the Priestess.

'Well I'll visit with your High Priestess?'

Idris didn't respond, she continued to Ophelia's room and knocked on the door. 'Time to leave.'

Ophelia opened the door. 'Idris. Is there a High Priestess?'

'I don't know.' The girl suddenly seemed young and even a little afraid.

'How can you not know if you have a High Priestess?'

'It is not my place to explain. I'll pass your request on to the Senator. He'll address your questions. I can't help you.' She scuttled off without a word, leaving Ophelia with a puzzled look and both women alone to make their way to the carriage themselves.

'That was strange!' Ophelia nodded after the Priestess.

'Something isn't making a lot of sense Ophelia. Icris just told me that the Order has been dabbling in politics and that she doesn't know who the High Priestess is. Culaan told me there has been a split in the Order and the Senator leads a faction.'

'Something to ask the Senator this evening then? He will have to give *you* a straight answer. You are the chosen one after all.' Ophelia giggled and wrapped her arm through Ariela's. 'Too many secrets in this place!'

'I agree. I asked to see the training ground, that's what started this whole discussion. Apparently, there isn't one and the Senator has been playing politics, using the Priestesses as weapons. How long has the Order been disrupted like this?'

The pair reached the carriage and the footman opened the door and helped them inside.

They settled into place and waited to begin moving before continuing their conversation. 'Let's focus on the amulet for now.' Ophelia suggested as the carriage moved out from the estate.

'Culaan told me the amulet is a hooked cross.' She drew the object in the air. 'Does that mean anything to you?'

Ophelia frowned, trying to recall all the artefacts she'd been taught about. Finally, she shook her head. 'No, maybe Hilderic knows something. Can we risk asking him about it?'

'I don't know. He seems to keep his head buried in the sand when it comes to his father and politics.'

'He is off with the fairies.' Ophelia laughed at an unknown jest. Ariela frowned at her friend. 'You can't tell me you haven't worked it out yet?' Ophelia nudged her friend in the arm.

'I have no idea what you are talking about.' Ariela was just about to pry more information from her friend when the carriage stopped and the door opened. It was Hilderic's smiling face that greeted them.

'Ladies. I thought rather than bore you with more time in the palace, we might take a tour of Carthage.'

The Prince hopped up into the carriage and called to the driver. 'To the harbour.' He pulled the door closed and took a seat next to Ophelia.

'I'd like to show you my father's ship. It's magnificent and the dock area is thriving with local people and markets. It's all very exciting.'

****

Culaan watched the Prince jump up into Ariela's carriage and leave the Palace grounds. He pushed his mount forward, following the King and his personal guard out of the marshalling yard as the carriage rolled past.

'Where are we going?' Genevieve whispered as they began to trot down the cobblestone laneway. The sound of the horses' hooves made further discussion impossible.

There were at least twenty soldiers with the King and Culaan wondered why they had been asked to join the trip today.

The Captain of the guard had not wanted them along. Roderic was still being sullen toward them. He went out of his way to make sure Culaan and Genevieve knew he didn't like them.

They travelled out of Carthage, toward the south and along the top of the ridge that overlooked the ocean. The sky was clear, the sun warm and the ocean was an impossibly blue colour.

Culaan nodded for Genevieve to see what he was seeing and she smiled knowingly. They had grown up in the woods, surrounded by tall green trees and dark, fertile soils. The barren, rocky slopes and the sandy beaches were foreign, but just as beautiful.

They had moved at a slow canter for over an hour, dropping back to a walk now to rest the horses.

'I heard Roderic mention something about a meeting of the Catholic and Arian Priests. Maybe the King is planning peace talks.' Culaan smiled as he picked up their earlier conversation.

'He wants Rome out of Carthage. The feud between the religions fuels his cause. He won't be brokering peace anytime soon.' The pair rode at the back of the formation, keeping their distance despite the continual disapproving looks from Roderic.

They followed the King's Guard into an old fortress. There were two tall towers vigilantly watching the ocean, but the stonework was worn and the wall was in disrepair.

As they rode into the courtyard a Priest dodged out of the way of the King's horse. More Priests could be seen walking along the covered entrance way.

The King's guard drew rein and the Captain called for them to dismount. A small stable boy took the King's reins while the Captain threw his to the closest soldier.

'This shouldn't take long. Tend the horses and listen for my signal.' Roderic's expression was pinched but his eyes held a strange glint. The soldier nodded and waved for the men to follow the King's mount.

The King turned as Genevieve and Culaan dismounted. 'Give your horses to one of my men. You will accompany me inside.'

'As you wish.' Culaan took Genevieve's reins and handed them to the last soldier as he moved by, his own horse walking on loose reins.

The siblings exchanged glances as they walked into the old fortress. The walls were peeling where plaster had begun to decay. There were no expensive murals or rugs on these walls. Whatever riches this place possessed had been sacked many years ago.

They entered the main hall to find rows of wooden tables lined with uncomfortable looking bench seats, all full to capacity with robed men. On the one side, men wore white robes with a large gold embroidered cross on the scarf that hung around their neck, while the other side, all the robes were dark red with black or white scarves.

Two men with tall hats sat at the head of a table on each side, both equally distanced from the dais, which the King now approached.

'I've called this meeting today to bring the Arian and Catholic clergy together. It's time you knew exactly where I stand on all this bickering over religious semantics.'

A hush fell on the room as all eyes watched the King. Culaan leant against the stone wall, his arms crossed and his manner relaxed as he and Genevieve observed the proceedings.

The King's nephew, Gunthamund sat to the left of a long table on the dais and a man Culaan didn't recognise, sat to the right. There were two chairs between them which the King and his Captain now approached.

Before the King took a seat, he waited. Both Priests with the tall ornately decorated hats stood. The sound of scraping benches followed as each Priest rose to his feet. The

King nodded, a smirk turning the tips of his mouth as he and Roderic were seated. All the Priests remained standing until the two men with the fancy robes and hats sat.

Culaan watched Gunthamund. His eyes drifted to the man seated on the other side of the King but they did not speak.

The King carried on conversing casually, as though the meeting was boring him. 'The Catholics have two weeks to leave Carthage or convert to Arianism.' The man beside the King whom Culaan was yet to recognise, gasped.

'Your Highness. Such an action could bring Rome to your door step.'

'I appreciate your counsel Senator, but Rome is presently occupied with the Goth horde. I don't think they will be bothering my kingdom any time soon.'

The man puffed out his cheeks and looked past the king to Gunthamund. The shrug was barely perceivable but Culaan noticed it.

'But your Highness. Freedom of religion is paramount. Surely, you don't want to stifle the beliefs of half your subjects?'

'*I'm* the one providing their prosperity Victorian. I have no need to explain myself to them.'

Culaan knew what the Senator must have been thinking. Huneric was providing for his people, for the local economy with the spoils of the Roman church. The Warrior felt a little sorry for the man. There was no way to win this argument.

'Any Priest who has not accepted Arian doctrine will be exiled, or worse.'

The murmurs that had started with the King's speech were quickly becoming louder protests. Roderic stood and drew his sword. He whistled and the King's guard flooded into the room from two different directions.

'I'm past coaxing this Catholic scourge from Carthage. Convert, or leave and men of Rome, leave empty handed or die.'

The King rose from his seat and left the dais, followed by Gunthamund who refused to make eye-contact with the Senator.

Chapter 22

People scattered as the carriage made its way down the wharf toward the King's black and sinister looking ship. The sails were furled, but the flags swayed softly on the light summer breeze.

Ariela opened the door and jumped out of the carriage almost before it stopped. The footman didn't even have time to jump down to open the door. The cry of birds, the hum of people talking, the smell of food cooking was overloading her senses and she felt free for the first time since she arrived.

Ophelia followed her with a grin from ear to ear and the Prince struggled to keep up. 'Ladies. It really isn't safe to wander these streets without an escort.'

'We are fine Huneric.' Ariela waved over her shoulder. 'If only he knew,' she whispered secretly to Ophelia.

'Ladies. Are you hungry?' A round man, with a rough beard but friendly eyes held up a roll full of juicy meat and Ophelia was the first to head in his direction.

As soon as Ariela arrived, Matias spoke quietly. 'I met a handsome friend of yours the other day.'

Ariela knew instantly that the food stall owner spoke of Culaan, but although Culaan said he had a friend in Carthage, he hadn't had a chance to say who. She decided to remain cautious.

'Really. I don't know many people here yet, except the Prince of course.' Matias looked over her shoulder as the young man pushed his way through the thick crowd of people, a look of mild anxiety on his features.

'Do you think you can shake him loose and meet some people I think you'd very much like to know?'

Ophelia looked at her and shrugged. Neither of them could sense anything dangerous about the man. 'Ariela. Please don't do that again.' The Prince looked pale as he dabbed at his nose with a handkerchief that neither of the girls had realised he was carrying.

'The smell a little much for you Hilderic?' Ophelia teased knowingly.

'Can't you smell the fish?'

'Yes, but it isn't that bad. I think the palace is making you soft.'

'The palace has nothing to do with it.' He smiled as understanding passed between Ophelia and the Prince. Ariela frowned, knowing she was missing something.

'We should carry on. Where to next Hilderic?' Ariela asked and nodded for Ophelia to lead the way. She looked at the street stall merchant, then back at Ariela before hooking her arm through the Prince's.

'Yes, what other wonderful sights can you show us?'

'I don't think we should……' The Prince's voiced trailed off as Ophelia dragged him deeper into the thong of people buying food and other wares on the dock.

'My friend hasn't mentioned you so why should I slip away with a stranger? You could be planning on abducting me for ransom.'

'Touch my arm. Sense whatever you need Priestess. I'm no threat to you.'

Ariela sucked in a quick breath. How did this man know what she was?

'Things are escalating fast. You need to know what's going on. Culaan doesn't seem to have brought you up to date. I think I need to.'

'The Prince will send out a search party the moment I'm out of his sight.' As if he heard her, Hilderic turned and sought her out with his eyes. She smiled and mouthed the words, *I'm coming*, before Ophelia drew him on.

'Can you travel the ethereal?'

'For goodness sakes, who are you?' Ariela was taken aback.

'Touch my arm. I'll show you a place. Meet me there tonight. You can bring a friend if it makes you feel better.'

Ariela didn't hesitate. She reached out and took the food from Matias, holding his hand firmly. A vision of a laneway past a tavern came to her. She opened her eyes and nodded.

'I'll see you there, but be warned, travelling the ethereal is child's play for me. I'll not make an easy target if you are planning anything.'

'I wouldn't do anything of the sort your Highness.'

Ariela moved away, taking a bite from the delicious meat roll as she pushed past a tall warrior with golden hair and leather armour. He reminded her of Culaan.

The Vandals must have been descended from Culaan's people. She absently wondered if any of them had Druid powers like Morrigan. She missed the woman's counsel. Growing up and taking responsibility was turning out to not be as easy, or as much fun as she had thought it would be.

'You spoke to the merchant a long time.' Hilderic tried to get another look at Matias but he was gone.

'He was very nice. He was talking of folklore and spilling tales of local magical history.'

'Magic. Don't let my father hear you speak of magic. Between him and your uncle, they both have no tolerance for such things.'

'Whyever not?' They moved through another laneway, away from the smell of fish. The scent of lemongrass and something sweet and spicy filled Ariela's nostrils and she was quickly distracted. 'Oh my. What is that smell?'

They found a dark-skinned little man with a cloth wrapped around his head mixing bottles of oil. He sat on a mat with beautifully shaped, carved wooden vials spread out in front of him. A small cork kept the liquid inside, but the wood had absorbed the smell and it seeped from the material and into the air.

'Here, let me get one for you. You pick a smell. I'll have this one for myself.' Ariela raised an eyebrow at Hilderic's choice, but Ophelia only grinned, that same knowing grin she expressed before.

Ariela lifted two up to her nose before deciding on the fruity smelling one. It was spicy, sweet and she could almost taste dried date in the air when she breathed it in.

Ariela and Ophelia carried on, while the Prince paid the seller. 'What was that all about?' Ophelia whispered.

'He knew who I was. He said he wants to meet. I'll take Culaan with me tonight.'

# Chapter 23

'You two,' the King pointed to Genevieve and Culaan as he left the old fortress, 'follow the Senator. I have no doubt he will be packing his bags the moment he gets back to Carthage. I need some leverage to keep him close at hand. Kidnap his niece. He won't dare send word to Rome if we have her.'

Culaan nodded, but inside, his mind was reeling. 'As you wish my lord.' They both turned to find their horses being led by two of the King's guard.

They mounted and rode from the old fortress at speed. As they moved over the crest, out of sight of the King they slowed.

'I don't like any of this Culaan.' The Huntress looked over her shoulder to make sure they were not being followed. 'I think the King plans to make us his assassins. I'd rather be fighting with his guard than sneaking around murdering people in their sleep.'

'I agree, but we need to stay in the King's favour to be close enough in case we get a chance to retrieve the amulet. Ariela seemed to believe it was important.'

'Maybe if we kidnap Ariela, she will be close enough to get the artefact herself?'

Culaan shook his head. 'I don't think so Genie. She told me she can't use her gifts near it. We need someone close to the King, maybe his son or nephew. Did you notice how Gunthamund was looking sideways at the Senator the whole time?'

'All I noticed is what an arrogant shite the King is. He brought all those Priests together just to scare the life out of them. He could have brokered peace. He told us he doesn't care about the religious differences. He wants the Roman Priests running.'

'I think he has succeeded in his wish, but what he really wants is for them to leave all their wealth behind. Let's find Ariela and we can work out what the best option is from there. She might know more about the amulet by now.'

****

A flurry of activity greeted the girls as they returned to the Estate. 'What is going on? Ariela questioned Idris when she found the Priestess packing bags in her and Ophelia's rooms.

'The Senator has to return to Hadrumetum.'

'Why the rush?'

'The King has given the Catholic Priests two weeks to convert to Arianism or face exile, or worse.'

'And that affects the Senator how?'

'This is an attack on Rome, not just on Catholics. The Senator is a representative of Rome. If the King exiles the Priests, it's only a matter of time before he might act against the Senator.'

Ariela had to admit it made sense but she had no intention of leaving Carthage, with the King and his amulet still here. 'I need to see Victorian now.'

'He is busy.' Idris fussed over the clothes she was packing, but didn't look up.

Ariela could feel her frustration rising. She'd played the Senator's games long enough. It was time to remind him why she was here and it wasn't to do his political bidding.

'I'll see him *now* Idris. Or I'll be leaving *now*. You decide which would disrupt the Senator more?'

Idris stopped what she was doing and took a slow, measured breath.

'You know something isn't right about all of this, don't you?' Ariela had her hands on her hips now and she was staring the woman down.

'I just do what I'm told.'

'I thought you were a Shiloh Priestess? Why are you packing my clothes and doing the Senator's bidding like a common servant? Why is the Senator using you to play with politics instead of doing what my mother created the Order to do?'

'Things have changed since your mother created the Order.'

'Yes, and they are going to change back. We were trained to fight evil… not get involved in political or religious disputes. How long has this being going on?'

'I'll go find the Senator.' Idris went to move, but Ariela slammed the door shut with a burst of air before she could reach it. Ophelia had flung herself on the bed and was now belly down, her head in her hands, watching the scene with amusement.

'You'll answer my questions. Who took over after my mother died?'

Idris's shoulders dropped and she slid down the closed door knowing too well that it was useless to try and open it against the Priestess's powers.

'I don't know the history that far back, but it wasn't a woman.'

'Did my father die the same time as my mother?' Ariela's heart began to thump in her chest.

'I really don't know. You will have to ask the Senator.'

'Move.' Ariela barked the command and Idris jumped to her feet. With the flick of a wrist the Priestess flung the door open once more and stormed through.

Ariela ran down the stairs and followed the noise that swept through the courtyard below. There were servants doing the Senator's bidding, running back and forth with trunks of more than clothing. The Senator was taking everything of any worth with him.

'Your Uncle has gone mad,' the Senator was yelling at Gunthamund who sat in a deep, soft chair in the Senator's study.

Gunthamund saw Ariela approach and nodded in her direction. Victorian spun round, his eyes wide. 'What are you doing here? You don't come into my study unannounced!'

Ariela stuck her tongue in her cheek trying unsuccessfully to bite off the words that were on her lip. 'How dare you.' She pushed the air around her and forced the Senator into the seat alongside Gunthamund. 'I want some answers and I want them now Senator.'

Gunthamund began to rise but Ariela forced him back with a surge of power. 'You stay right where you are.'

'The King has an amulet. Where did he get it?' The Senator opened his mouth to speak, but Ariela held up her hand and he stopped.

Gunthamund focussed on the petite girl before him and frowned. He tried to rise, but couldn't. 'What witchcraft is this?'

'Not the damned Arian or Catholic kind, that's for sure. Answer my question.'

'It was his father's.' Gunthamund needed no further encouragement. Ariela nodded, accepting his reply.

'How did my mother die?' This question she directed to Victorian 'No more lies.'

'How would I know?' The Senator became defensive.

'Tell me what you *do* know then. Who led the Order after my mother died?'

'A Priest called Nathaniel.'

'Nathaniel, my Uncle's advisor?'

'Yes, I believe so.' Victorian spoke tentatively, sensing Ariela's mood.

'My mother told me about that slimy little man and none of it was good. How is it that a man leads an Order of Priestesses?'

'Because men make wiser decision, without their emotions getting in the way. Like now. You are letting your emotions control you Princess. You are a prime example why women shouldn't lead.' The Senator puffed out his chest and rose from his chair. Ariela let him.

'So why is it that God gifts the Priestesses and not the men who *lead* them?' Ariela was on the verge of letting her emotions get the better of her now, but she remained focussed.

'We have different gifts.' The Senator sounded defensive.

'Like manipulation, like pushing your moral code aside for wealth, like putting your own ideals before others? Yes, I can see why God would put you in charge.' Ariela pursed her lips and nodded with feigned seriousness.

Gunthamund smiled at her sarcasm.

'You run off to Hadrumetum. I'll keep Idris here with me and train her to be a *real* Priestess, not your slave. How many others have you pulled from their true path?'

Idris and Ophelia had been watching the exchange from the study entrance. Ophelia resisted the urge to clap her hands together with excitement, but Idris was harder to read.

'There are no others here today, but I know where he keeps them.' Idris moved forward and joined the Priestess

'Keeps them?' Ariela snarled. 'Show me.' She released Gunthamund from her hold and turned to leave, grabbing Idris by the arm on the way.

'Why do you want to know about the amulet?' Gunthamund asked before she could leave.

'Because it's evil and fighting evil is what the Priestess Order is supposed to be doing, not picking sides in adolescent bickering over whose religion is right or wrong.'

Ophelia moved from the doorway to allow Ariela room to pass. Idris shook her arm loose of the Priestess's grip. 'I told you I would show you willingly.'

Ariela nodded. 'Wait here. I need to get something.' She ran up the stairs, collected her apparently empty bag and lifted it over her head and shoulder, returning quickly to Ophelia and Idris.

It was getting late and the Priestess realised as she left the Senator's estate, she had no coin and no transport. Moving three people through the ethereal was something she had never tried before and didn't want to start right now, especially with no idea of where she was going.

Chapter 24

Culaan could sense Ariela was close. He opened his mind to listen for her voice. *Culaan. Thank goodness.*

'What's wrong?' Culaan spoke out loud and Genevieve raised an eyebrow.

'Ariela?' she whispered. Culaan nodded and focussed on her voice once more.

We need to meet now. Where are you?

'Nearly to the estate.' Genevieve shook her head. 'What? This talking in my head is strange. I'm working on it.' His sister laughed.

I left the estate a little disorganised. No horses, no carriage. We are walking to the wharf.

'Meet us at the food-stall that serves roast meat rolls. You can't miss it. Follow your nose.' Culaan pushed his mount into a slow canter and Genevieve followed.

I was there today. I know the place.

Within a short time, Culaan passed the Priestess on the road but there were too many people around to offer her a ride. Even if he was supposed to be kidnapping her, he wouldn't do it in plain sight and the last thing he needed was for one of the King's guards to report he picked her and her friends up without a fight.

He reached the wharf and dismounted, leading his horse to a railing that overlooked some of the smaller boats tied to the dock. Genevieve tied her reins around a post and followed him to Matias's stall.

The round little man smiled as they approached and held up a roll for each of them. 'We have friends joining us

Matias, but they can't be seen with us.' He reached for the roll and took a bite. 'You recall the woman I spoke to you about?' He spoke with his mouth full.

'Yes, yes. I met her today. I introduced myself.'

Culaan looked to Genevieve who shrugged. 'That should make this easier.' She smiled

'Hopefully. Can you bring them to meet with us somewhere safe?'

'You remember the blue door?' Culaan nodded. 'When they arrive, I will bring them.'

****

'Was that Culaan?' Ophelia asked as they moved out of the way to let two horses canter by.

'It was. He will meet us down at the wharf. He can't exactly stop and pick us up. He isn't supposed to really know us that well.'

'Who is Culaan? How do you know where he'll meet us?' Idris joined the conversation uninvited.

'It's a long story. You were told when we arrived that we were not alone. The Senator knew we had friends who were likely working for the King. He might not be so pleased about it now though. Culaan and Genevieve are quite deadly and if the King has it out for the Senator, chances are our friends are tasked with the deed.'

'How much do we trust her?' Ophelia looked past Idris to her friend.

'She's a Priestess.'

'Yes and I am right here. I can speak for myself you know.' Idris pursed her lips and looked from Ophelia to Ariela with obvious irritation.

'Yes, but you have been misled. Start talking and we can decide how much we can share with you in return.'

Ophelia had her hands on her hips and was uncharacteristically firm.

'I can take you to where our training ground used to be, but it was dismantled before I began working with the Senator.'

'How long ago?' Ariela's feet were killing her and she stopped mid-stride to pull off her light slipper and remove a stone. 'These shoes were not made for walking outside.'

'Ladies of your status don't usually walk anywhere Ariela,' Idris smiled.

'I have no status Idris. The Order treats all of us the same, besides, I like my food too much to sit around and be waited on. It has been weeks since I trained properly. My muscles are growing weak.'

'Why do you need strength with the power you have? You shut that door in my face and kept it shut with ease and the way you put the Senator back in his seat, I've never seen that much power.'

'My powers are getting stronger, but I've met others with such power and being able to combine them with physical strength has saved me more than once.'

'What else do you know? You said you could take us to the others.' Ophelia focussed the Priestess back on subject and Ariela smiled at her friend.

Ophelia was the ideal friend. She didn't mince words and always told the truth no matter how much it might hurt.

'I know your parents didn't die of natural causes. It is only a rumour but the man who took control of the Shiloh Order had them killed.'

'Nathaniel. Victorian said it was Nathaniel.' Ariela almost spat the man's name.

'Who is he?' Ophelia moved around Idris to put her arm around Ariela's shoulder, sensing her unease.

'My Uncle's adviser, the Priest of the first temple of God, but he was a broken man. My mother told me what he did to my aunt and uncle. My aunt was nearly stoned to death for infidelity because of him.'

'And he led the Order after Ariela's parents died?' Ophelia turned to Idris for confirmation.

'So it is said. We have not been led by a Priestess in any histories I have heard.'

'So that is why you said you didn't know your High Priestess. That's terrible.' Ariela put her shoe back on and sighed. 'Well we will be led by a Priestess again before I leave here Idris. Of that you can be certain.'

The wharf came into view and Ariela stopped to take it in. She had seen the harbour from the hill as they had walked with Titus, but seeing the magnificent structure up close was breath-taking.

A huge circular harbour lay in front of them. Ariela looked at Ophelia whose mouth was open. 'I have never seen anything like it.'

The walls were stone and stood tall above the ships that were docked in bays, like the spokes of a wheel on a carriage. Outside the structure, the long wooden wharf hosted the taverns and food stall where they had visited earlier that day.

Ariela led the way past the tall black ship that had been moved from the wharf and docked inside the circle ship yard. It was clear the wharf was where the town folk congregated, while inside the large, protected harbour, wealthy merchants and royal ships took pride of place.

The stout little man saw them approaching and met them outside his stall. 'You must come with me ladies. I will take you to your friends.' He spoke quietly, but over the hum of voices and laughing sailors, no one could possibly have overheard.

'What is going on? I thought I was taking you to see,' Idris hesitated, 'you know.' The Priestess's brow creased with her confusion, but she followed when Ariela gave her a *do as you are told* look. 'This isn't what I agreed to.' Idris mumbled under her breath.

'You can go back to working with the Senator if you prefer. How you can after what you've been told is beyond me, but it's up to you. No one is forcing you to stay.' Ophelia put her hand on Idris's shoulder as she spoke.

Ariela stopped. 'Make up your mind now Idris. We take you no further than this if you are still undecided.'

Idris looked at the bearded stall holder and wondered what she could share aloud. 'I don't want to be his servant any longer. You lead, I'll follow.'

Chapter 25

'I don't have the time or the patience for Gunthamund right now. Send him away Roderic.' The King rolled the amulet between his fingers. *Listen to him.* The voice in his head insisted.

The King's nephew pushed past the two guards on the door of the dining room. 'You will want to hear me out Uncle. You have traitors in your midst.'

Hilderic watched his cousin. He was a tall man, with golden hair and broad shoulders. He had been the older brother the Prince had never had for many years, but because of Hilderic's lack of interest in politics and his womanising, they had grown apart.

'You are the only traitor I know of Gunthamund.' The King stayed seated at his table, calmly eating his meal as though his nephew were a mere inconvenience.

'I have spent time with the Senator, yes, but not as a traitor. The honour of the Vandal kingdom is my only concern Huneric. You know I would never do anything to jeopardise that.'

'No, you would just undermine me.' The King took a sip of his watered wine and placed the fine glass back on the table before him.

Hilderic took his glass and sat back in his chair to observe, as his cousin pulled a chair out and took a seat uninvited. The King waved a servant to fill all the glasses, including one for Gunthamund and sat back to wait.

'He's been plotting your death. That should not be a surprise. But his niece isn't really his niece and there is more.'

Gunthamund took a sip of wine, allowing his news to create the desired agitation in the King.

'Did you know this Hilderic?' The King looked at his son whose eyes were already wide with surprise, answering his father's question. The boy could never keep his feelings hidden.

'She is a witch. I came from the Senator's estate a short while ago. Victorian was packing and jumping ship like the rat he is, but his niece refused to leave.'

'That hardly makes her a witch.' Hilderic defended his new friend, but his voice lacked conviction.

'No. But she pushed her hand toward me and I was nailed to my seat like the Christ himself. No matter how hard I tried, I couldn't move.'

The King drew in a frustrated breath and drank from his wine glass. This time emptying it in one long mouthful.

'She had her *uncle* in the same position and she was not exactly speaking as a niece would to an elder. She left with her friend and the Senator's serving girl.'

The King studied Gunthamund carefully. The voice in his mind tried to speak to him, but he pushed it back. Roderic stood by the door, awaiting his orders eagerly. The man loved any chance for violence.

'Who are the traitors you speak of? Ariela has been a guest, and it sounds like an ungrateful niece, but that does not make her a traitor to me, only her Uncle. What are you not telling me? You really think she is a sorceress of some kind?'

'I told you what she did. What other explanation is there? The Senator called her *Princess* and they spoke about *Priestesses* and the *Order*. She has spent many hours with Hilderic. What has he learnt?'

'I doubt gardening and sight-seeing have unveiled any palace secrets Gunthamund. I think you are desperate to redirect my anger from you.'

'She is a witch uncle and she asked about your amulet.' The King's hand moved to his chest instinctively and Hilderic could have sworn his eyes flashed red.

'How could she know of my amulet?'

'As I said, a traitor in your midst. Who, I cannot say.'

****

Ariela could feel Culaan was close, but he ran around the corner and swept her into his arms before she even came into view. She laughed as he kissed her cheeks and held her close, his face buried in her hair.

'I'm fine Culaan. You can put me down.' She could feel the warmth of his body and didn't want him to let her go, but everyone was watching and this really wasn't the time.

'I'm never letting you out of my sight. Tell Raziel, next time we leave and arrive together or the deal is off.' Culaan whispered in her ear.

'I'm not sure it's that easy, but we can try.'

Matias was smiling from ear to ear as Ophelia moved past the couple to greet Genevieve.

'Has he been as big a love-sick puppy as I'm guessing?' Ophelia nodded her head back toward Culaan and the Huntress laughed aloud.

'Absolutely. Impossible to deal with to be honest.'

Idris looked around suddenly feeling the odd one out. She fixed her gaze on Matias who lifted a shoulder in resignation.

'Come. We must go.' Matias moved down the laneway and opened the hidden doorway. Ariela and Ophelia looked on wide-eyed for only a moment, but Idris was rooted to the spot.

'It is safe. We've been here before.' Culaan led Ariela by the hand, but she stopped to wait for Idris.

'If Culaan says it is safe Idris, it is. Come on.' The Priestess waved her new friend to join them.

'I have not seen magic used in Carthage since I was a small child. Now, it is all around me, you and now this man.' Idris nodded to both Ariela and Matias.

'If you grew up with magic and do not fear it, then you are a Priestess, yes?' Matias moved back around the steps and patted her on the shoulder. I will show you where you truly belong. The Senator has deceived you child.'

Idris nodded and followed the group into the narrow passage beyond the hidden opening. The Priestess looked overwhelmed as Matias led them through the great hall, full of Priestesses, training, laughing, eating and sharing fellowship.

'How long have you been here?' Ariela could feel power all around. 'How do you remain hidden?'

'I'll answer your questions Princess. I need to share something with you first. Follow me.' Matias led the small group through another hallway, under the stone arch and into his private rooms.

'Make yourselves comfortable.' Matias waved a hand indicating he didn't mind where they chose to sit.

'Ariela. Your arrival has been foretold.'

'So I've heard. The Senator said the same thing.'

'Yes, no doubt. He was once a part of our Order, but he lost his way.'

'I don't mean to sound sceptical, but from what I've seen so far, you may have all lost your way.' Ariela sat on a divan, Culaan falling alongside of her with a grin.

'Matias has been very helpful,' the Warrior offered in his defence.

'What did you need to tell me Matias?' Ariela didn't try to hide her irritation. The Carthage political turmoil was beginning to annoy her and she was still upset about her discussion with the Senator earlier.

'The King has an amulet. Culaan tells me you know of it.' Ariela nodded as she looked to Ophelia. Matias followed her glance.

'You must be the Relic Seeker.' Ophelia looked suspiciously at the man.

'How do you know of me? I was never a part of the Shiloh Order.'

'Your history is known to us.'

'How? Who told you about Ophelia?' Genevieve hadn't found a seat, instead she sat on the edge of Matias's desk, her arms folded over her chest.

'Before you answer that question Matias. Who leads the Shiloh Order now?' Ariela couldn't contain her curiosity any longer.

'I do my best Princess. The Order has been fragmented for many years. The Senator led before he took our most highly trained fighters on his political rampage. The Priestesses who remain are very young.'

'Does the Senator know of this place then?' Ariela sat forward, ignoring Culaan's arm still draped over her shoulder.

'No. I don't believe he does. When the Order broke, and we found the traitors,' Matias nodded to Culaan 'I found a new place for those who were left.'

'Who created the hidden doorway then, if you have no trained Priestesses? Who trains the Priestesses with gifts?'

'I do Ariela, with guidance of course.' Matias looked above to acknowledge the divine realm. 'Maybe you are here for the amulet or maybe you are here to restore your mother's order.'

'I've seen the effect the amulet has on the King. I must retrieve it, but my gifts are blocked when I am near it. Do you know why?'

'It is possessed.'

Genevieve chuckled and Culaan frowned. 'How can a piece of jewellery be possessed and what with?' the Huntress continued to smile at the idea.

'I've only heard stories, but my aunt and my mother had encountered demons before. I've never heard of an object being possessed.'

'It is a Mare spirit. Have you heard of such?' Matias looked around the room, gauging the young faces that surrounded him.

'Why didn't you say something earlier?' Culaan moved to the edge of the divan, on alert.

'It wasn't the right time. I told you the amulet was evil. The Mare spirits can invoke horrific dreams in those they plague. They feed off the anger of the host.'

'That explains quite a lot. I've seen the King go from charismatic to frightening in a heartbeat.' Ariela touched Culaan's arm to calm him. The Warrior moved back into his seat, sighing.

'The amulet must be taken from him. Over time, it brings madness to anyone who wears it.' Matias moved around his desk and leant upon it.

'The King sent us to kidnap Ariela. Some sort of plan to manipulate the Senator.' Culaan held Ariela's hand apologetically.

'Yes, and I said it might present the perfect opportunity to get the amulet, but Culaan didn't think it was safe.' Genevieve began to pace Matias's study.

'My powers are limited near the amulet. I don't think I can get to it without the King knowing.'

Culaan watched Idris wring her fingers as Ariela spoke. 'You look uncomfortable.' He focussed the Priestess with an intense stare and she grew more agitated under his gaze.

Idris put her hands on her cheeks as she blushed. 'I've been working with the Senator for so many years now. I'm not sure I can still do it. He focussed so much on the Priestesses fighting, he never encouraged any gifts.'

'What can you do?' Ophelia sat down next to Idris and tapped her on the knee to get her to look at her.

'I told you I had no powers. Well that isn't entirely true. I've not practised for a long time, not since I was small, but I used to be able to stop people moving.'

'Try now. Can you stop one person or everyone?' Culaan stood up next to Genevieve who was now standing in front of Idris.

She looked up at the two formidable warriors before her and shrunk back, suddenly feeling vulnerable.

'You two oafs. You're crowding her. Get back.' Ophelia stood to shield the woman. Idris was the oldest there besides Matias, but she seemed young and overwhelmed by the two Gaul warriors.

'Why didn't you tell us?' Ariela sat down alongside Idris and spoke quietly to her. 'You said you had trained as a fighter. Why did no one encourage your gift?'

'The Senator needed a bodyguard, someone to watch over him as he played politics in Carthage. He wasn't interested in my gifts, in fact, the Catholics believe the Priestesses' power is evil, that the Order is an abomination to God.'

'Did you know of this Matias?' Ariela challenged.

He nodded. 'I did. It is one of the reasons Victorian left the Order.'

'Yet he believed in it enough to expect me to arrive. We'll discuss all this later. For now, we need to work out what we are going to do.'

'If we take you to the King, hopefully we'll be able to move around without suspicion.' Genevieve offered and Culaan opened his mouth to protest.

'She's right Culaan. If you don't take me, the King will think you have broken your agreement.'

'But if you can't use your gifts, there will be no one there to protect you.' Culaan reached for Ariela's hand and she moved to join him.

'Culaan, it's what I'm here for. I didn't take this quest, leap through time to stay safe. I did it to serve a purpose.'

'Yes, but being bait isn't a sensible thing to do.'

'I won't be bait. You, Genevieve and Ophelia will watch over me and Matias, will work with Idris on her gift. I've got an idea. Trust me.'

Chapter 26

The small group left Matias's hidden fortress through the regular blue door. Genevieve pushed Ariela roughly and Culaan tried unsuccessfully not to cringe. He led Ophelia, her hands bound with a leather tie, the same as Ariela.

They rounded the corner at the end of the alleyway as Roderic rode up with more than twenty soldiers at his side. Culaan tensed as the Captain smirked. The expression caused chills to run down his back.

'Ah. You found her. Good. The King is waiting.'

'What are you doing here Roderic?' Culaan pushed Ophelia forward, Genevieve did the same with Ariela who looked over her shoulder, an eyebrow raised in question. The Huntress didn't react, instead she pushed the Priestess again, adding a growl for good measure to convince Roderic.

'Just making sure you complete the task. The King was wondering what was taking you so long. Lead the way.' Roderic waved his hand for Culaan to move past him, but he didn't miss that the Captain's hand hovered over his sword.

The hilt of Roderic's weapon struck Ariela as he rode between the two warriors and their prisoners. The Priestess crumpled to the ground as horses reared and turned, knocking Culaan and Ophelia to the ground.

Genevieve pulled her bow from her shoulder and stepped back to make room, but a guard to the left of Roderic pushed his horse forward and the Huntress ran for cover back down the alleyway, reluctantly leaving Ariela on the ground unconscious.

'Ophelia. Get to Ariela.' Culaan drew his sword. He didn't hold back the light, which blinded the horses and caused two to rear and throw the riders to the cobblestones. Bones crunched and screams sounded as the men were trampled beneath their frightened mounts.

The alleyway exploded into a flurry of horses, riders, weapons and bright lights. Genevieve had made her way to the top of the stairs before the blue door. She took aim and shot the rider closest to Ariela. The Priestess still lay on the ground unconscious, horses trampling close to her helpless body.

Culaan threw himself over Ariela, taking a hoof to the middle of his back, the wind was knocked from his lungs and he was pushed from the Priestess.

Ophelia grabbed Ariela's arm with her bound hands and began to drag the Priestess to cover, but a King's guard leapt from his horse and pulled her from her feet. She hit the ground hard, the guard still on top of her.

Roderic moved in, dodging an arrow which struck his ear. Blood ran down his cheek as he kicked Culaan aside and jumped to the ground. He lifted the petite Priestess easily. Ariela didn't stir as he threw her over his horse's neck and vaulted to its back.

The sound of hooves on stone echoed in the alley as the blue door opened behind the Huntress. Genevieve loosed another arrow, but two of the King's guard followed their Captain and the arrow thumped the last soldier from his horse as the bright, magical arrow struck.

Culaan tried to vault to a riderless horse, but six of the King's guard remained. All were still mounted and all blocked the alley, their horses prancing with nostrils flaring.

'Culaan, inside. *Now.*' Matias yelled.

Culaan turned to see Genevieve helping Ophelia to her feet. He looked at Matias, the horses before him and the back of Roderic who was now too far ahead for Genevieve to strike with an arrow.

A guard moved his mount forward as if to challenge the Warrior. He was too angry to control his emotions now. His sword grew bright as he drew on every ounce of his mother's power. He'd had no time to put it to the test before arriving in Carthage and he had no idea what to expect, but he threw his hand in the air the same way he'd seen Ariela do before. The rider was thrown through the air, the sound of bone crunching loud enough for all to hear as he hit the side wall with force.

'*Now* Culaan.' Matias begged as two more horses moved forward to attack.

Culaan swung his sword, the weapon humming loudly. People opened their windows above the alley to see what all the noise was about, but closed them quickly at the sight of the King's men and the shining weapon.

All five remaining guards pushed their horses forward. Culaan was too enraged to focus, his sword slicing the air threateningly. All he could think about was Ariela, unconscious, flung over Roderic's horse.

An arrow swept past his head and took the first soldier in the chest, but then all motion ceased, including his own. His sword hung in the air, sparking and hissing but not moving. His eyes bulged, as did those of the four remaining guards, the fifth floated in the air, an arrow in his chest, his eyes shut with pain and his arms outstretched to catch the fall that hadn't come.

'Culaan, now. Come now!' Matias called again. The Warrior tried to move and at first, his legs wouldn't obey, but then his arm moved, his sword completed the arc it had begun and the movement nearly threw him off balance.

He felt his legs move and turned to see Idris standing on the top of the stairs, her arms held out in front of her, her eyes closed tightly as though the scene was too gruesome for her to see.

The Warrior moved slowly at first, but quickly gained speed as he moved up the stairs two at a time. He lifted Idris from her feet as he followed Genevieve through the still open doorway. The Priestess opened her eyes and gasped, as the men before her began to regain control of their limbs.

The door slammed as Matias pulled it closed behind them, placing a thick wooden plank in place. He muttered a few words that Culaan couldn't understand and then sighed with relief before turning to face the Warrior.

'Now what do we do?' he asked as Culaan began to shake with subsiding adrenalin.

Chapter 27

'We'll have to keep her unconscious. She started to awaken and sent two of my guards flying before I knocked her out again. Gunthamund is right. She's a witch.' Roderic carried the Priestess into the palace through the west entrance.

'Take her to my room.' Hilderic instructed, but the King's Captain frowned at the request.

'Weren't you listening to me? She's deadly. The dungeon is the place for her.'

'Father. If you want to use her as a bargaining tool to manipulate Victorian, she'll need to be well cared for.'

'The boy has a point Roderic. I'm not so much interested in using her to control the Senator, but I knew all along there was something powerful about Culaan. If he wants her so much, he'll have to come and get her.' The King grinned.

'Take her to Hilderic's room. We'll keep her sedated and locked up inside.'

'How do we do that?' The Captain began moving toward the Prince's quarters, Ariela draped over his shoulder. As much as he wanted to see Culaan put down, he hated witches. They used powers he didn't understand and couldn't control. The quicker they killed her the better, as far as he was concerned.

'I have herbs that might work.' Hilderic opened his door and watched as Roderic placed Ariela on his bed. 'I'll need to go and get a few things.' He turned and left the room, closing the door behind him.

'The boy is soft.' Roderic offered, but the King only shrugged.

'He's not next in line. That will be Gunthamund's problem not mine.'

Hilderic returned with a handful of flowers. Roderic barely suppressed a laugh.

'How are flowers going to keep her knocked out? I think I'll just sit here and hit her on the head every time she moves.'

'You can't do that. You'll likely kill her you idiot.'

Huneric grinned at his son's unusually assertive manner.

'You like this one?' He looked at his son and waited for the reply.

'It isn't like that. There is something about her. I can't explain it.'

'It's called lust boy. I thought you'd never discover it.' Roderic chuckled, but Hilderic didn't answer.

He tore the flowers from the roots and placed them on the table next to his bed. He found his mortar and pestle and placed the roots in the stone dish and began crushing them into a paste.

'We'll need hot water,' he said, to no one in particular. The King and Roderic exchanged glances and Roderic moved to the hall to find a servant.

The water appeared and Hilderic placed the crushed roots in the hot water and stirred it slowly, gently blowing on it to cool it down. 'You can go now. I'll keep her sleeping.'

'What do we do about the mercenaries?' Roderic spoke as they left the room. 'Culaan fought like a lion when I tried to take the girl.' Hilderic listened to their voices as they drifted off down the hallway.

'Ariela. I'm so sorry.' The Prince lifted the Priestess's head and put the cup of liquid to her lips. He gently tipped the potion down her throat, making sure not to choke her.

****

Ariela floating above the palace... the building was transparent and she could see her body laid out on Hilderic's bed, the Prince tending her with great care.

She looked around; the sky was not bright blue as she had expected. It held the haze of the Void that she had travelled in her astral form, but it was different, somehow less real, less tangible than she had ever seen it.

She flew down through the building to stand beside Hilderic. He stopped dribbling the liquid into the mouth of her earthly body and looked over his shoulder as though he sensed her presence.

The Priestess moved toward him and touched his shoulder. Her hand passed through him, but the Prince shuddered and spun round.

You can feel me. Ariela spoke as she would when talking to Culaan in her mind.

'Ariela?' The Prince looked at the still form before him and touched her cheek 'How are you awake?'

I'm not. It's hard to explain.

'Gunthamund thinks you are a witch and Roderic seeks to harm the mercenaries who protected you. I thought you must have known them. The way Culaan looked at you at our dinner the other night.' Hilderic smiled at Ariela laying on his bed.

Hilderic. I need your help. Can you find Culaan? Can you tell him I am safe before he does anything stupid?

'I'm not sure you are safe Ariela.' The Prince looked around to make sure no one could see him, but even if they

152

could, he was talking to a sleeping girl afterall. He chuckled to himself. 'This is crazy. How are you speaking in my head?'

Have you heard of the Order of Shiloh? Ariela had concluded that if the Senator had shared who she was with Gunthamund, then the Order wasn't as secret as she had first thought.

'Only vaguely.'

I'm one of the first of the Order. I don't really have time to fully explain, but your father possesses a dangerous amulet. You've seen it?

The Prince nodded but said nothing.

I've been tasked with retrieving it, so that the evil it possesses can be contained. Culaan and my friends will be trying to figure out how to get it now that I've been kidnapped, but maybe you can get it for me?

'Why would I do that?'

Because if you don't, you father will likely go mad with the power it holds. Don't make up your mind yet. Find Culaan, speak with him, with my friend Ophelia. They will explain everything.

'I'm not a brave man Ariela. I'm supposed to be here, guarding you.'

The sedative the Prince had given Ariela took hold and she was drawn once more back into darkness.

 **Chapter 28**

'That was spectacular,' Genevieve laughed as she hugged Idris, who kept her hands at her side, wondering what to do with them.

'I'm going to kill Roderic, with my bare hands if I have to,' Culaan snarled as Matias led them back to his study.

'What do we do now?' Ophelia looked at Genevieve as they entered Matias's study once more.

'They knocked Ariela out. They must know she has power! But how?' Culaan rubbed his chin, frustration evident in his voice.

'Ariela used her powers on Gunthamund and Victorian before we left the Senator's estate. Gunthamund must have told the King and Roderic. That's why Roderic came after you.' Ophelia dropped into the divan with a hard landing, her fancy dress laying out over her legs like a bedspread.

'I need a change of clothes.' She looked to Matias who nodded he'd find her something.

'Idris. Can you control that power yet?' Matias took a seat behind his desk and leant on one elbow, impatiently awaiting an answer.

'I think so.'

'She certainly did very well just then.' Genevieve grinned at their new friend with genuine warmth.

'I'll find reinforcements. We'll need help getting Ariela out and finding the amulet.' Matias drew the Huntress back to the matter at hand.

'I don't think anyone but Ariela will be able to touch it.' Ophelia offered. 'Only her gift will be powerful enough to hold the amulet and not be affected by the spirit within.'

'Are you sure?' Matias rubbed his chin as he considered the Relic Seeker's revelation.

'Almost certain.' Ophelia insisted. 'She might not be able to use her power around it, but I've seen her handle all the artefacts we've found and they respond to her. She has control over them somehow.'

'Then we need to get organised. Culaan, you, Genevieve and Ophelia go to the palace and see if you can find a way in. Watch the servants, the guard change, anything that might offer an opportunity to gain entry.'

Culaan nodded and moved to the door, anxious to find Ariela.

'What will you be doing?' Genevieve asked over her shoulder as she followed her brother.

'I'll be preparing the handful of trained Priestesses I have, to do what they've been waiting to do for years. Fight evil.' Matias grinned with the excitement of youth and bounced off his chair.

Idris looked confused, but Matias slapped her on the shoulder. 'You are trained to fight girl. You have talents we have yet to fully explore. You'll do just fine.'

****

It took only a few carefully asked questions to discover where Roderic had found Ariela. He arrived in the alley but it was deserted, except for two King's guards who were doing a terrible job of trying to remain inconspicuous.

The Prince noticed them before they saw him. He returned to the main thoroughfare and headed around the back of the building. The Captain of the guard was not stupid and more guards waited in the narrow passage that led to the back of the building.

The Prince turned to leave but a flutter of fabric caught his eye. A blue cloak flashed on top of the bridge that joined two rooftops to each other over the narrow walkway.

The Prince followed the cloak. He was sure he'd seen Ophelia wear it the day before. He kept looking up, making sure not to lose sight of it, but one moment it was there, the next it was gone.

He circled around the front of the buildings, looking up and down the street and into every portico or shopfront he could find. The hand that grabbed his shoulder was large and rough and Hilderic found himself staring into the crystal blue eyes of his father's mercenary.

'Culaan. Ariela sent me.' The Prince turned away, with his eyes closed as the Warrior raised his fist. He heard the sound of flesh on flesh, but there was no pain. He opened his eyes to see Genevieve holding Culaan's fist in the palm of her hand, only inches from his face.

'What do you mean she sent you?' Genevieve spoke as she pushed Culaan's fist aside, glaring at him to get a grip on himself.

'Well it sounds strange now that I think about it, but you have to believe me. She was unconscious.' Culaan grabbed the Prince by the shirt.

'Culaan stop it. Let him speak.' Genevieve slapped the Warrior's hand away. She turned to Ophelia. 'See what I've been dealing with!'

Ophelia smiled but Culaan continued to glare at the Prince.

'Go on.' Ophelia coaxed.

'They were going to put her in the dungeon.' Culaan let out a low growl and the Prince pulled on his collar with his finger, trying to get some air.

'I suggest you get to the point of what Ariela told you.' Genevieve encouraged the Prince with the nod of her head to her brother.

'Yes, well she wasn't awake but she spoke to me. Honestly. That's what happened.'

'She can do that.' Genevieve scrunched her lip and looked to Culaan for confirmation. The Warrior took a deep breath and stepped back from the Prince.

'Go on,' the Huntress nodded.

'She told me to find you. That she had to get my father's amulet and that you would convince me to help. I don't like the idea, but maybe you can explain why it's so important.'

'Have you noticed a change in your father's behaviour since he began wearing it?' Ophelia moved forward, her long blue cloak floated behind her, revealing a short tunic that had replaced her formal long and rather awkward dress.

'He's worn it since Grandfather died.'

'Has he changed since then?' Ophelia pushed.

'A little. Mainly in his dealings with the Catholics. He used to approve of them practising their religion, now he persecutes them.'

'Exactly so. The amulet is influencing him, as it likely did your Grandfather.' Ophelia started moving. 'Come on. We have to get to the Palace.'

'Wait. What are you going to do?' The Prince moved to quickly catch up with the trio.

'We needed a way in. Maybe you are it.' Genevieve linked her arm in his and Ophelia did the same on the other side. The Prince's eyes widened with nothing short of fear.

# Chapter 29

'I've posted guards outside the orphanage. As soon as anyone leaves, we will know about it.' Roderic paced as the King poured himself a cup of wine. 'My men said that Culaan and Genevieve had magical weapons.'

'Any of you believe them?' The King carried on as though the news were pure fiction. He had no intention of sharing with Roderic what his inner voice had sensed all along.

'Send word to the Senator that we have his niece. Culaan will come to find her, I have no doubt, and we might be able to kill two birds with one stone.' Huneric took a long, slow sip of his wine and swilled it around his mouth, savouring the flavour before letting it trickle down his throat. 'This is magnificent.' He raised his glass in salute.

Roderic watched the dark red wine swirl in the glass. It was the finest Rome could offer and no doubt anointed holy wine. The Captain of the guard knew it would never touch his lips as the King always kept the sacred wine for himself.

'Well, what are you waiting for?' Huneric waved his hand to shoo his Captain out of his office. 'Find Hilderic will you. I sent for him, but someone said he had left the Palace to fetch more flowers or some such nonsense.'

Roderic bowed and turned to leave, but he stopped. 'What if the girl is not Victorian's niece?'

'If what Gunthamund says is true, we'll have to kill her before she wakes up, but not before Culaan and Genevieve come for her. I want that traitor dead.'

Roderic bowed and left the King.

Huneric touched the amulet at his neck. *She's dangerous. We must kill her now. The warrior can wait.*

The King dismissed the voice in his head. It had been growing more persistent of late. In the back of his mind, he knew he should confide in a Priest, but the voice kept telling him that to do so would open him up to attack from his nephew or worse still, the Romans.

****

Hilderic bit his lip as he entered his father's study. The room was large and formal and even without all that was going on, he always found it intimidating. Or was it his father he found overwhelming?

'Finally! Where have you been?' Huneric spat the words with frustration, his hands folded across his chest awaiting an answer.

'Collecting more valerian father.' The Prince was surprised at how steady his voice sounded. 'I don't keep a lot of it around usually.'

The King pursed his lips and nodded. 'The girl still sleeps?'

'Yes.' Hilderic did not elaborate. His father could smell a lie in his sleep.

'Gunthamund believes her to be a witch.'

'I heard him. I was there.' It wasn't the first time the King had missed his son's presence. He hated hunting, loathed politics and had no interest in women. He knew his father wondered whatever he might be useful for.

'Roderic thinks we should kill her, that she isn't Victorian's niece at all?'

The Prince wondered if the statement were a question, but surely not. His father never sought his counsel.

'He seemed very attached to her.' Hilderic offered, wanting to delay any possible harm to the woman he now knew to be a Priestess. The idea still had his mind swirling. The Order was an ancient fairy-tale, folklore to both the Arians and the Catholics who spoke of it with great reverence but with no real belief; like a lot of the religious drivel that went on within both churches.

If they knew what he really desired out of this life, both religions would stone him to death, so he held no love for Arian or Catholic.

'Roderic has sent word. Let's see if the Senator comes out of hiding to help her! Either way, I'll get that treacherous mercenary. He obviously wants to protect her.'

'What do you want of the Senator?' Hilderic desperately wanted to talk about anyone but Culaan in case he betrayed the man accidentally. He was not born for the game of politics.

'To delay Rome knocking on my door of course. I'm massing more soldiers with the Catholic gold and I need a little more time to be ready. Once Rome finishes with the Goth invasion, they will turn their attention back to Carthage.'

'Why not broker peace again? Why go up against the strongest army in the world?'

'Do you forget I was their hostage?' Huneric snarled at his son.

'But you married mother, a Roman. Why is it so hard for you to bury your hatred?'

'I came back to rule the Vandal nation after your Grandfather died. I wanted to ignore my father's lust for battle against Rome, but I can't Hilderic. They will come for us as soon as the Goths fall to them. It is only a matter of time.'

Yes. Exactly. You must strike against them first. Kill the Senator. Banish the Catholics. The King shook his head, but Hilderic saw the soft, red glow before it vanished.

Ophelia was right. His father used to honour his mother's heritage. He used to focus on Carthage and the commerce of the region, but not anymore.

'You know how little I understand of politics father. I'll return to Ariela if that is alright with you?'

'Yes, yes, go.' Hilderic bowed to his father and left the room, stopping just outside to take a slow, deep breath. His heart was racing; his mind a flurry of questions.

Chapter 30

'Ariela. Can you hear me?' Ophelia sat on the large four-posted bed and touched her friend's cheek.

Yes.

'Good. Hilderic says you will wake up soon. When you do, you must pretend to remain unconscious.'

I understand.

Hilderic opened the door and entered his room. 'You have to go now. Before someone recognises you.'

'I doubt anyone will.' Ophelia had been a maid before. She knew no one took any notice of serving staff.

'Roderic has returned. He'll come for Ariela soon.'

'Why?'

'The Senator has refused to come back to Carthage.'

'No surprises there. I'll go find Genevieve and Culaan.'

'Has she awoken yet?'

'No, but she knows what to do when she does.'

Ophelia opened the door a crack and peered out. The hallway was empty, so she slipped out and pulled the door closed behind her. She dusted the painting and the balustrade railing as she made her way down the hallway toward the servants' stairwell.

Two maids and a courtier moved past her never even bothering to make eye contact. Ophelia was about to enter the spiral staircase that would take her to Culaan when she felt the presence of the relic.

The touch of the hand on her backside made her jump, but her heart leapt to her throat as she spun around to find the King, his eyes leering at her cleavage.

'Oh you are a pretty one. New by the look of it.' The King pushed her against the wall and cupped her breast firmly in his hand as he began sucking on her neck.

Ophelia's mind was racing. What if he recognised her? What if he expected more of her than she was willing to give?

The King pushed his hand inside her top and for a moment she thought he would have his way with her, but the sound of someone clearing their throat stopped him.

'My Lord. Sorry to disturb you.' Ophelia recognised the voice and kept her eyes cast down and face tilted to the ground. Maybe the King didn't know who she was but there was a very good chance that Roderic would.

'Yes, I know. The witch.' The King pinched Ophelia's nipple between his thumb and forefinger. 'You. Join me in my bedchamber tonight.'

Ophelia curtsied when the King finally removed his hand and didn't rise until Roderic moved down the hallway with Hilderic.

She took a quick look over her shoulder as she stepped into the servants' stairwell, only to find Roderic taking a backward glance in her direction. There was no way to hide her face, so she smiled shyly, hoping he didn't recognise her.

Once inside, she stood with her back against the cold stone wall, taking ragged breaths and trying desperately to shake off the disgusted feeling in the pit of her stomach.

She moved down the stairs until she reached the lowest level. Culaan was pacing the floor, while Genevieve was picking her nails with the tip of her sharp hunting knife that she usually wore on her thigh.

'You took your time.' Culaan spat accusingly.

'The King took a liking to my breasts.' Ophelia grabbed both and lifted them with her hands to emphasise her point.

'Bastard.' Genevieve put her knife back in the scabbard. 'I'll cut his manhood off for that.'

'Are you alright?' Culaan changed his tone. 'Did he recognise you?'

'Not a chance. Naked possibly, but I doubt the King would recall my face from dinner. Roderic on the other hand, I think he might have.'

'Damn. We had better hurry then. That man is a sneaky rat if ever I met one.' Culaan drew his sword, but kept the light from glowing.

'They were just going to get Ariela when I left. Hilderic said the Senator had refused to come back to Carthage and that they would likely try and kill her now.'

'Then let's get moving. We can't wait for Matias.'

'We have to. Ariela is the only one who can pick up the amulet and she is still waking up.' Ophelia insisted as the trio took the stairs back up to the main level.

****

Huneric and Roderic entered the Prince's room. Ariela lay on the bed, Hilderic stood at the window.

'You should see this.' The Prince pointed out the window as his father and the Captain moved across the room.

Outside, in the main entrance courtyard stood twelve hooded figures, with one bearded, round little man standing out in front, robed but his hood lowered.

'I'll bring the girl. You find out who they are Roderic.' The King lifted Ariela over his shoulder, her head thumping against his back. Her limp body bounced as he made his way to the door.

'Hilderic, come with me. I'm afraid this girl's time is up and this is your opportunity to finally make a man of yourself.'

Roderic laughed aloud. 'You want him to have his way with her before he kills her?'

Hilderic's eyes grew wide with fear. 'I, I…'

'What boy. You afraid of putting your *manhood* in a *woman* or killing her?'

'That's enough Roderic. Focus on your work and leave my son to me.' The King moved through the still open door, not waiting for Roderic, who was still chuckling to himself as he followed.

'Come on pork chop. Don't look so shocked. You think your father doesn't know what you are? If you weren't a Prince, you'd be dead already.' Roderic pushed the Prince in front of him and patted him on the backside, laughing louder as Hilderic jumped forward.

# Chapter 31

Roderic left the King and Prince in the main throne room and walked out onto the entrance terrace. The man he recognised, known to the Captain as the orphanage owner, a local merchant and a spy for whomever paid the most.

'Matias. To what do we owe the unpleasant honour of your visit today?'

Matias moved forward, bowed slightly and raised his head with a smile. 'I'm here to see the King.'

Roderic laughed, the sound loud and forced and lacking any humour. 'He is a little busy right now.' The image of Hilderic being forced to rape the witch before killing her created arousal. He was only sorry he would miss the fun himself. Raping witches was his favourite pastime.

His mind drifted to the woman the King had been fondling in the hallway. He kept trying to figure out where he had seen her but his memory was not cooperating.

'It really is very important. It's about the woman you took hostage earlier today.'

Roderic pulled his attention back to the man before him. He studied the robed visitors, realising only now that they were all women.

'She will be finding her end very soon Matias. This is none of your concern. We have no need of your *intelligence* on this occasion.

'Well, we had best introduce ourselves more formally then.' Matias turned to face the robed women and all pulled back their hoods at once.

Roderic scanned the faces, some plump, some beautiful, but all women and all no threat to him. 'Get away with you Matias. I'm too busy to be bothered with you and your orphaned girls right now.'

The sudden movement of all twelve women set his heart racing. The one on the left drew a sword, then one in the middle drew a staff. Two women in the second row back pulled bows from under their robes.

How on earth did they get past the guards with weapons?

'Guards!' the Captain called, drawing his weapon as the courtyard erupted with movement and the gates slid down to the ground with a thud. The only guards at Roderic's disposal were the ones inside the Palace. No one else would be entering from the barrack which stood outside the Palace gates on the other side of the parade ground.

Culaan stepped out from a pillar on the terrace and tapped Roderic on the shoulder with the tip of his drawn sword. 'You and I have a score to settle my friend.'

Roderic spun round as Culaan stepped back, allowing himself room to manoeuvre.

'Don't play with him too long Culaan. We need to get to Ariela.' Genevieve drew her bow and began shooting at the guard tower on the left of the gate. Two soldiers fell to the ground, arrows perfectly placed in the neck of each.

The two archer Priestesses began peppering the right tower in the same manner. One guard tumbled from the battlement, an arrow in his chest.

'I'll kill you, then I'll rape that witch of yours you scum.' Roderic circled his weapon over his wrist and moved around, crouched ready to fight.

Culaan allowed his weapon to surge. A sound like a hive of bees grew louder and he swung the sword through the air.

'You keep them busy. Idris and I will help Ariela. Ophelia, show us the way.' Matias moved past Culaan and Genevieve with Idris following quickly behind.

'Are you ready for this?' Ophelia asked Idris, noting her nervous movements.

'I have to be, don't I?'

Genevieve took a knee and continued to pepper soldiers who got close to the remaining Priestesses fighting in the courtyard below. She marvelled at their skill. None used magic that she could sense, but all fought with precision.

A tall blonde girl used a staff that spun faster than the naked eye could see. Another short, rounded girl no older than sixteen flipped and spun like a palace acrobat, belying her stature with remarkable speed. Each tumble ended with a guard unconscious or too dazed to fight.

****

'I'll not kill her father.' Hilderic stepped back as the King threw Ariela down on a divan to the side of the main hall. She bounced so hard, she nearly landed on the marble tiled floor.

'You won't rut with her; you won't kill her. What kind of King will you make?'

Hilderic took a deep breath. 'The loving and intelligent kind.'

Huneric laughed so hard, he nearly snorted. 'You are a naive boy. King's rule with fear. Only fear keeps the masses from rising up and taking control.'

'No father. Prosperity for all. If everyone is fed, loved and has a home to keep them warm then they have no need for revolt.'

'Every man seeks power boy. The sooner you learn that, the better off you'll be. Now take the girl, then kill her.'

Hilderic shook his head. 'Most men want a loving family, children, music, art, entertainment and great food. Most men aren't like you father. They don't seek the sort of power you crave.'

'Take her now Hilderic!' The King moved toward his son, his face set in an unnatural snarl and he grabbed the Prince by the shirt.

'This isn't you father. This is the amulet.' Hilderic spoke softly, looking into his father's frenzied eyes.

The King let go of the Prince's shirt and slapped his son so hard that he was knocked to the floor.

'Please father. Don't do this.' Hilderic struggled to rise, and leaning on one knee, he took a deep breath.

'What has this witch told you of my amulet?' *Kill her now. I told you to kill her.*

The King turned to Ariela and looked at her dark skin, her dark almost black hair and wondered who she really was. *Kill her.*

He pulled his dagger from the scabbard as Ariela opened her eyes.

'You don't have to kill me. I know the spirit of the amulet speaks to you. It wants me dead because I can contain it when no one else can.'

Ariela reached out with her talent but there was nothing. Her power was useless when the King was this close, but she knew she needed to give her friends time.

Chapter 32

'Who are you?' Roderic could feel his heart beating wildly in his chest. The power of Culaan's weapon vibrating so loudly that his whole body felt like it was being shaken.

'Your worst nightmare come to life.' Culaan's sword connected with Roderic's again and sparks leapt into the sky.

'Stop playing Culaan! We need to get to Ariela. Matias might need our help.' Genevieve surveyed the courtyard. The Priestesses had everything under control now and there were no more guards in the towers or on the walls for her to pick off with her arrows.

Culaan raised his hand and a burst of energy hit Roderic in the chest with enough force to take the wind out of him. He gasped for air but kept his footing and his sword in his hand.

He advanced hard and fast, but Culaan side-stepped the thrust, his own weapon striking Roderic in the side of his shoulder. As the sword connected, the smell of burning flesh filled the air.

Roderic cried out, but Culaan didn't slow his advance. He spun around, his sword moving in an arc from high to low over Roderic's back. The Captain's armour was no protection for the Warrior's weapon, which sliced through the black leather, cutting deep into flesh and bone.

Roderic slumped to his knees as a flaming arrow struck him in the chest, his eyes bulged, his lips moved, but no words were uttered as he fell sideways onto the marble terrace, a trail of blood pooling on the shining white stone.

Culaan looked at Genevieve as she shouldered her bow and drew her sword. 'What? You were taking too long.' She shrugged and leapt into a sprint, heading through the main entrance and on toward the hall where the hysterical screams of a man could be heard.

****

Ariela saw Ophelia enter the main hall, as Hilderic started screaming for his father to stop thumping him on his back like a child mid-tantrum.

The King swept him aside like a leaf in a storm and Hilderic slid to the ground, a look of pure horror on his face as he made eye contact with Ariela.

It's alright Hilderic. My friends are here.

The Prince's tear-filled eyes opened wide as he spun round to see two robed figures and Ophelia running toward him. He scurried on his backside to the side of the room, trying his best to become invisible.

'Stop Huneric!'

The King grabbed Ariela by the arm and yanked her to her feet. He pulled her around, forcing her back against his chest, trapping her behind her own arm. She wriggled trying to free herself until the tip of his blade touched her throat and she stopped moving.

'You need to stop him Idris.' Matias whispered as he moved forward, trying to distract the King.

Ophelia watched helplessly, not really knowing what she should do.

'Huneric. Do you know who she really is?' Matias took a step forward, while Ophelia slipped toward the side of the room unnoticed.

'Stay where you are Matias or she dies. I don't want to hear your fairy tales right now. Where is Roderic?'

'Being taken care of.'

'What does that mean?' Huneric looked past Matias, who had come closer despite the King's warnings.

'Culaan and Genevieve. They aren't who you think they are either.'

Huneric shook his head, as if trying to clear his mind of something. 'It's all gone so wrong.'

'I know. Let Ariela go. She is a Shiloh Priestess Huneric. A prophecy of old.'

The King shook his head again. 'Don't be ridiculous.' He adjusted his grip of Ariela.

'She is father. I know she is.' Hilderic wiped the tears from his cheeks as he tried to convince his father.

'She is a witch.' The King pushed the blade into the skin of Ariela's neck and the Priestess winced.

'Idris.' Matias didn't take his eyes off the blade.

The King's hand stopped moving, the blood that had begun to trickle down Ariela's throat slowed and ceased its path.

Matias turned to see Idris standing with her eyes closed and her hands in the air. She was shaking with the energy required.

'I can't …. hold him…. long. The amulet…. is powerful.'

Matias ran to the Priestess and pried the knife from Huneric's hands. The King's eyes were wide, but his lips were frozen in time.

Ophelia helped Hilderic to his feet and tried to think of something she could do to help. She looked for a weapon, anything.

Ariela was trapped in the King's embrace, neither she nor the King could move.

'You'll need to let them move a little Idris. The King has an iron grip on Ariela.' Matias pulled on the King's arm as Ophelia tried to unwrap Ariela's hand from his.

'I can't. If I let... him go... even a little, he will... be free.' Idris was on her knees now, struggling to hold the King under control. The man's eyes were darting from Ophelia to Matias as they battled to free Ariela.

'I'll need to retrieve the amulet myself.' Matias moved toward the King's neck, gently trying to feel around Ariela's dark thick braid.

'You can't. It will kill you.' Ophelia pleaded.

'We don't have a lot of choice.' Matias opened the King's shirt; the amulet was trapped behind Ariela's head.

'No!' Idris screamed, as she lost control and fell to the floor.

Ariela moved slower than the King, but without a weapon he was unable to cut Ariela's throat, instead he took her neck in his one free hand and began to choke her.

'Get back.' The King took a step away from Ophelia and Matias, dragging Ariela with him. 'Or I will kill her.' The sound of Huneric's voice hissed like a serpent. 'You will not take me.'

Culaan and Genevieve burst through the door. Genevieve reached for an arrow only to find her quiver empty.

'I told you to leave Roderic to me.' Culaan's confidence fell away as he tried to push the King with his new-found magic, but it wouldn't respond. Ariela's feet were off the floor now, thrashing in the air as she held her weight against his arm with both her hands. The King squeezed her neck harder as Culaan moved into the room.

Culaan took another few steps towards Ariela, his weapon held at the ready. He willed the blade to life but nothing happened. The Priestess was losing consciousness and he tried to force the fire that usually buzzed and hissed into existence.

'Now you die Priestess.' The King's voice still hissed.

Hilderic jumped to his feet and ran at his father, pushing him with his hip and shoulder as hard as he could. Matias joined the struggle as Ariela fell to the floor, her body limp, her face impossibly pale.

Ophelia reached the Priestess in time to stop her head from hitting the floor.

The three men struggled on the marble tiles as Culaan and Genevieve ran to join them. Idris had regained enough strength to get to her hands and knees, but she struggled to rise.

Culaan reached Ariela and cradled her in his arms, willing her to breathe. He rubbed her chest and touched her cheek, the bruises on her neck already showing.

Ophelia shook her head at him, tears running down her face.

Genevieve, Hilderic and Matias continued to struggle with the King as Culaan kissed Ariela on the lips, holding her tightly, tears glistening in his eyes.

He placed her gently on the ground and stood, walking over to the flailing group as though in a trance. He drew his weapon, without the need for any added druid magic. He placed the blade against the King's throat.

'Move and you die.' The words were flat and lifeless. 'No. Actually, please move. You need to die.' Culaan pushed the blade to emphasise his point and the King stopped struggling.

'It matters not. She's the only one who could have caused me any harm.' The voice still hissed and Hilderic frowned at the unrecognisable sound.

Genevieve took a leather lace from her hair and tied the King's hands behind his back.

Ophelia remained with Ariela's body, the Priestess's head cradled gently in her lap.

Genevieve looked at Culaan's pale face. She reached for his arm but he pulled away, the light gone from his blue eyes.

'What do we do with him now? He's still the King.' Matias asked Hilderic as though the boy should hold the answers.

'He lives, there is no Vandal history to dethrone a King. I'll need to speak with Gunthamund.'

Culaan moved away from the talk of politics and lifted Ariela into his arms. Ophelia stood and wiped her face with the sleeve of her robe.

Idris moved over and touched the Priestess reverently. She recoiled slightly, looking at Culaan, a spark of hope in her eyes.

'You felt something?' Culaan searched Idris's expression as Genevieve wrapped her arm around the Warrior's shoulder.

# Chapter 33

The room was quiet as a round black hole appeared in the corner between two large pillars. No one noticed the frail little man with his bare feet and loin cloth until he appeared in front of Ariela.

Culaan snatched Ariela away from the man's scrawny hands, but he only chuckled good naturedly.

'The Princess lives.' He handed Ophelia a bag and smiled before touching Ariela's face gently and returning to the black hole everyone now noticed.

Ophelia held the bag and smiled with great relief. She reached inside and pulled out the star that was surrounded by symbols. She placed it in Ariela's hands and wrapped her cold fingers tightly around the object.

'What are you doing?' Culaan hugged Ariela protectively.

'It's alright. Trust me. Idris. I might need your help, yours too Matias.'

The Priestess and Matias came closer as Culaan placed Ariela back on the divan. 'What do we do?' Idris looked at the amulet and touched it carefully.

'I have no power except recognising these artefacts. I'll need your help, all of you.'

'No!' The King began to struggle. 'You can't.' Culaan took his sword from its scabbard and approached the bound monarch.

'You can't kill the King.' Matias protested and Hilderic stepped forward to defend his father.

'After all he has done, you would protect him?' Culaan shook his head. 'Relax, I'm not going to kill him.'

Hilderic studied the Warrior's face and stepped aside, nodding. Culaan nearly laughed aloud, knowing there would have been nothing the Prince could have done to prevent his father's death, but he respected the bravery.

'You heard them. You can't kill me.' Culaan turned his weapon hilt first and smacked the King in the face with full force. The man's legs gave way and his body crumpled to the ground, landing awkwardly in a heap.

He turned as Genevieve laughed aloud and smiled, feeling a sense of hope returning. He joined Ophelia. 'What do we do?'

'You all have some sort of power. We need to focus it now.'

'On what?'

'On this star.' Ophelia touched the artefact. 'It was Ariela's mother's and when she holds it, it glows. It must have some connection to her.'

Idris was the first to place her hands on the Priestess and the star. 'I felt something. We must try.'

'No one is going to ask about the little guy who just came through a dark hole in the wall?' Genevieve grinned at the faces that circled Ariela. 'I'm guessing Ophelia is right. Let's do this.' Genevieve placed her hand on top of Idris's.

Matias did the same, with Culaan putting his hand on last.

'Think about how you invoke your power, channel it to the amulet.'

After a few moments of trying to focus his power Culaan sighed. 'It's not working. Nothing is happening.'

He looked up and saw the King, still unconscious on the floor. 'His amulet.' He took his hand from Ariela's chest and grabbed the King by the foot and dragged him past a chair, knocking Hilderic's head on the leg as he passed.

He walked through the doors and down the hall, dragging the King's limp body as fast as he could. 'Prince, come watch your father. If he wakes up, kick him in the head.' Culaan called over his shoulder and Hilderic moved quickly to assist.

Culaan returned, closed the double wooden doors to the room and ran to Ariela's side once more. He placed his hand back on top of the others and took a deep breath.

Culaan watched the Priestess's face, which had grown increasingly grey since she collapsed.

Raziel, if she survives, you and I are going to have a serious talk.

That is a deal Gaul.

Culaan chuckled aloud and Genevieve gave him a sideways look. 'I was just telling the Angel what I thought of him.' She raised an eyebrow. 'He answered.'

Genevieve grinned and focussed on the amulet.

The feeling of warmth spread through their hands and the star below grew hotter with every passing moment. If it was glowing, they couldn't tell below their hands.

Sweat beaded on Idris's face, but she focussed all her energy. Culaan ran his hand through Ariela's hair as he prayed that this would work.

****

'Missed me yes?'

'Narayana. I have missed you *so* much.' Ariela wrapped her arms around the little holy man who had taught her about the hiding place in time and space and so much more.

'It's been months for you, but much has changed.'

Ariela looked at her hair that floated in the air like ribbons on the breeze. She knew where she was but was she dead?'

'Close to it.' Narayana answered her silent question.

'I'll see my parents again soon then.'

'No.'

'No?'

'Your work is not done child. The Angel calls you I've given your friends a gift. They call to you now. Listen. Follow your heart. Hear them.'

Ariela closed her eyes and opened them to daylight—to Culaan's smiling face—to his lips—to a feeling of warmth in her whole body.

Culaan lifted his lips from hers. 'I am so happy to see you,' he whispered.

'Did I pass out? I had the weirdest dream.'

'No, you died babe.' Culaan helped her to her feet, supporting her with his strong arm wrapped tightly around her waist.

Ariela rubbed her bruised neck. 'I need to get that amulet.' Where is the King? Did he get away?

'He isn't going anywhere. It can wait.' Genevieve assured her, joining the Priestess to support her on her other side by wrapping Ariela's arm around her shoulder and ducking lower.

'No. I don't think this can wait. Where is he?' She looked over her shoulder.

'He is in the hallway. His amulet was blocking us from reaching you.' Culaan began to lead the way out.

Ariela looked confused. 'We'll explain later.' Genevieve promised.

They opened the double doors to find Hilderic on the ground, sitting with a large wooden candlestick hovering over his father's head.

Culaan laughed. 'Just in case.' the Prince smiled back.

Ariela knelt next to the King and opened his shirt. She tentatively touched the crooked cross with the tip of her finger. Nothing. She smiled at Culaan who knelt alongside her, still unwilling to let her go.

I will find a way to fulfil my will.

Ariela smiled at the Mare spirit, the amulet balanced now in the palm of her hand.

Not while I breathe air and you can see. I'm pretty hard to kill.

# Chapter 34

'I'd like to come with you.' Idris wrapped Ariela in a hug. 'But you honour me. I won't let you down.'

Ariela turned the Priestess's hand over and found the burnt reflection of her mother's amulet permanently etched on the skin.

'You earned it Idris.'

Matias walked over and patted Idris on the arm. 'The King is back on his throne, but I'm not sure how long that will last. His nephew itches for the power.'

'At least the family won't have the amulet to fuel their ambitions.' Ariela sighed.

Hilderic moved toward Ariela, warily watching Culaan to make sure the big, blonde Warrior didn't mean him any harm. Culaan grabbed the prince in a big bear hug and rubbed his head with his knuckles. 'You're alright Hilderic. I'll let you give her a hug.'

'Let him? Who made you the king of me?' Ariela shoved Culaan, but her smile told a different story.

Hilderic wrapped his arms gently around Ariela and pulled her into a soft embrace. 'I was never interested in girls,' he whispered in her ear.

The Priestess chuckled. 'Ophelia told me as much,' she whispered back.

'I'll make sure the Order is supported Ariela. I owe you,' the Prince looked at Matias, 'them, everything.'

'You owe us nothing Hilderic. You are a gentle soul. You'll make a great king when the time comes.' Ariela saw Idris looking intently at her.

'Can we take a walk?' Idris asked and took Ariela by the arm. 'Do we have time?'

'Raziel isn't exactly one for great communication, but I can usually feel him as he comes near.' Ariela held up her hand for Culaan and Genevieve to stay where they were. Culaan scowled as expected, but Ariela calmed him with the touch of her hand on his chest.

The two Priestesses moved out of Matias's study and made their way into the training yard that opened into fresh air right in the middle of the underground fortress.

He had kept a lot hidden during her visit, but his motives were pure. The Shiloh Order had been in tatters, but Matias had done his best to hold it all together.

'I'm not sure I'm fit to lead.' Idris whispered, not wanting anyone to overhear.

'That makes you the perfect person for the role.' Ariela smiled at Idris who returned the gesture. 'Matias will help you. In time, you will be a wonderful High Priestess.'

'That just sounds so strange. We haven't had a High Priestess since...' Idris stopped herself mid-sentence.

'Since my mother. It's alright. She'd be very proud of you. No one expects you to be perfect, not straight away anyway,' Ariela teased. 'You need time to hone your own skills. I'm still learning and I was brought up in the Order.'

Ariela stopped and looked up at the sky above them. The sun was high and the training ground was surrounded by covered walkways and flowering shrubs. She was suddenly reminded of her own Shiloh and took a deep breath to stop herself from tearing up.

'Are you alright?' Idris put a hand on Ariela's arm.

'I don't think I've ever been better.' Ariela smiled. 'Gather the others Idris and bring them home. My mother wanted the Order to fight evil. If you remember nothing else of my visit, remember that. We don't fight for politics, or power. We don't do the bidding of kings or merchants or even our own leadership if it betrays that mandate. We do the work of God; the bidding of the angels and we fight evil.'

Idris hugged Ariela before they walked back to the group.

'It is time.' Ariela smiled as she entered the room. Culaan, Genevieve and Ophelia all nodded as the sun rose in the windowless stone walls of Matias's study, buried deep in the new Shiloh Fortress.

What Now?

If you enjoyed *Shiloh Rising*, I would really love to hear from you. You can leave a review with your favourite book retailer.

While you are waiting for the next instalment in *The Priestess Chronicles* series, why not download the first book in my complete first series absolutely free
www.atime2write.com.au

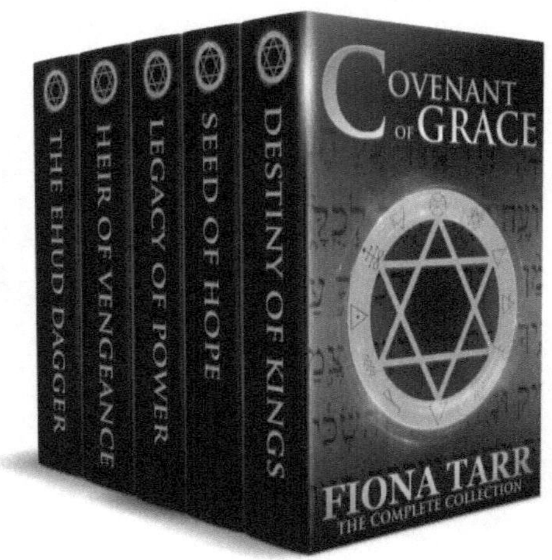

Dedication

This book is dedicated to anyone who has ever sacrificed their own wants and needs for the good of others and done so without expectation of reward in this life or the next. You are a rare and precious soul.

Thanks to my beta team George and Rachel. Your feedback is always awesome and helps to shape each and every story. Thanks to my cover designer Simon and my editor Adele. Love your work, both of you!

Books by Fiona Tarr

Covenant of Grace Series
Destiny of Kings
Seed of Hope
Legacy of Power
Heir of Vengeance
The Ehud Dagger Novella
The Complete Collection – all 5 books

****

The Eternal Realm Series
The Jericho Prophecy
Delilah and the Dark God
Reign of Retribution

****

The Priestess Chronicles
Call of the Druids
Relic Seeker
Shiloh Rising

****

All books are available from your online retailer, in stores or you can find the links on my website www.atime2write.com.au. I enjoy hearing from you, so please follow me on Facebook or Instagram. You'll be the first to know when my next book is released.

Thanks again for taking the time to read my work and I look forward to your enjoyment of more tales as they come to hand.